CHRISTMAS IN SHOTGUN RIDGE

MINDY NEFF

CHRISTMAS IN SHOTGUN RIDGE

Editor: Mary-Theresa Hussey

Cover Design: Melissa Storm/Sandy Novy Chvostal

For Joy—because your silliness and sweetness has truly brought joy into our lives.

And for Sue Phillips and Sandy Chvostal—best friends and writing pals. I couldn't do this without you! I love you both!

CHAPTER 1

*C*lay Callahan's heart slammed right into his throat. He had no idea what made him look in the direction of Cherry Peyton's pasture—he refused to think of her as Cherry Payne and was glad she'd taken back her maiden name when she'd buried her bastard of a husband. The town's folk might have believed her bruised cheek was from the accident. Clay figured different.

Still, the sensation he felt in his shoulder pulled his head right around, and his gaze zeroed in on Casanova. It was as though someone had given him a poke and shouted, "Look!"

He didn't take time to analyze spooky thoughts, because what he saw lying too close to that prize bull's hooves had his knees digging into the sides of his chestnut mare. He urged Ginger into a flat out run, praying—for what, he wasn't sure. The mare's hooves ate up the muddy ground. The land between Wyatt Malone's property and Cherry Peyton's was flat Montana prairie covered by patches of snow and very few trees. Cold air bit his cheeks, sliding icy fingers past the collar of his sheepskin-lined denim jacket.

As Clay neared the pen, he took off his hat, waved it in the air and yelled. "Ha. Go on now. Get the hell out of there."

The bull looked up, seemed to consider, then turned and lumbered away, glancing back just as Clay put the horse in a skid and jumped from the saddle. Anger surged through him. He wanted to put a bullet in the beast but knew Cherry would have his hide. She treated that bull like a pet rather than the dangerous two-ton animal it was.

Besides, Casanova was her livelihood. The only decent thing Wendell Payne had left her—besides the land.

He bent and gently scooped his hand under Cherry's fiery hair. Her name and hair color were a walking cliché. Both red. But man, she was beautiful.

And she held his heart.

Although he wanted to shout, his voice was gentle. "Hey, sugar. Open your eyes for me, now." Her skin was paler than usual. Freckles stood out on her nose and cheeks. Her lips held a tinge of blue. He had to get her off the cold ground, but he wasn't sure of her injuries—other than the bloody gash on her leg, which was obvious because of the huge tear in her jeans. It would take quite a blow to rip heavy denim this way.

Kneeling on the wet ground, he held her head and shoulders with one arm and fished out his cell phone.

Her eyes fluttered open. Blue. He could see the moment pain surged.

"Just hang on. I'm calling Chance." Chance and Kelly Hammond were the doctors in Shotgun Ridge. Since he and Chance had grown up together, Clay had his number in his personal contacts.

"No," she said. "Just help me sit up."

"Not a chance, tough girl." He sat on the muddy ground and shifted her head to his lap, smoothing sticky strands of hair away from her face. "What were you doing messing with that bull, anyway? I swear you treat him like a tame animal—and he's not."

"I know my livestock, Clay."

He snorted, his free hand gently caressing her cheek. "Just be quiet a minute."

She rolled her eyes, and he could see the effort it took not to cry.

Chance Hammond answered his phone on the second ring. "Where the heck are you, man? We're all over here at Wyatt's and—"

Clay cut him off. "I'm at Cherry's. Looks like she's been gored or stepped on by that damned bull."

"I'm heading for the truck now. Where, exactly."

"This side of Butterhill. By the pen where she and Wyatt keep Casanova."

"On it. Be there in a couple of minutes."

Clay tossed the phone down and barely winced when it landed in a patch of dirty snow. He glanced at her face. Pain lines etched her brow. "I can see the leg. Where else do you hurt?"

"Just my chest. I think I hit a rock when I fell."

"I could kill him."

"Oh, don't be so dramatic. Besides, it wasn't Casanova's fault. Something startled him. Maybe bit him, I don't know. I was laying out the salt lick and then next thing I know he's bucking. I didn't get out of the way in time."

Clay wasn't sure if he should try to attend to her wound—and he wasn't sure how he felt about her "dramatic" comment. He was relieved to see Chance's truck coming across the meadow. Cherry's property bordered Wyatt Malone's. When Wyatt had talked Cherry into selling him insemination rights

3

to the bull, he'd graded a road—which was pretty much a muddy path at the moment—that ran between his ranch and Cherry's, making it easier to get to the bull.

The doctor got out and grabbed a tackle box from the seat beside him. "Well, you two are missing some pretty good spiced cider and cookies." He kneeled and expertly assessed Cherry's condition.

She tried to sit up, but both men stopped her.

"Let me have a good look before you move," Chance said. "Besides the leg, what hurts?"

"Her chest," Clay answered automatically. "And she's got a cut on her head."

Cherry hissed out a breath, the corners of her eyes pinched. "I'm perfectly able to speak for myself. Something spooked Casanova. I didn't get out of the way in time, and he got me in the leg. I think I was trying to twist away and I landed on that rock." She gestured to a boulder the size of a small melon. "I can't tell if it's my chest or ribs that hurt."

"Hmm. Might have a cracked rib. We'll see to that in a minute. Hope you're not partial to these jeans." Chance took out a pair of scissors. "Sorry. Kelly says I'm scissor happy and should have more of a care for fine clothing." He grinned.

Kelly had been been a specialist in Beverly Hills before she'd come to Montana to practice medicine and raise her two little girls. Thanks to Cherry's uncle and his band of geriatric matchmakers, she'd not only joined Chance's medical practice, she'd married him as well.

"Cut away," Cherry said, then winced when denim and mud pulled at her torn flesh.

Clay glared at the doctor—who cheerfully ignored him.

Cherry ignored Clay, too, biting her lip and fighting to remain still. If she wasn't mistaken, she'd fainted when the bull had kicked her. That was a first. She'd endured a lot of pain in her life and had never gone down for the count. She didn't like the feeling of being out of control.

Chance poured a sterile solution over the wound, then manipulated her leg. "Hurt when I do this?"

Cherry nodded. Hurt was an understatement. She felt Clay's fingers against her hair tighten a bit. You'd think he was the one with the gash just above the calf.

"I won't know if it's broken until I take some X-rays. And this wound requires a lot more than a field dressing. I'm gonna have to haul you in to the clinic."

"Why don't you just bandage it up and we'll see if I can put weight on it?" The idea of paying for X-rays and an office visit sent her into a slight panic. Finances were tight this time of year. Who was she kidding? Finances were tight *any* time of the year. "I have more first aid supplies at the house. If you can help me get home I should be fine. No sense in taking unnecessary X-rays. I haven't even had a chance to sit up and assess what's what."

"Cherry, don't be stubborn. Chance knows what he's talking about. You should go to the clinic."

Cherry ignored him—as much as she could with his hard thighs beneath her shoulders. "Do you have the supplies in your kit to fix my leg wound?" she asked the doctor.

"Yes. It would be easier in my office, but I can manage it—provided there are no surprises when I get a better look and see if you can bear any weight."

"I don't see what the big deal is," Clay said.

Cherry looked at him. She didn't want to beg. And she didn't want to air her dirty financial laundry either. Something in her look must have gotten to him.

"Can I move her?" he asked Chance through obviously clenched teeth.

Cherry wanted to roll her eyes.

"Sure. Take her to the truck and we'll get her to the house —if you're sure," he said, this time turning to Cherry.

"I'm sure for now. You've got a party to get to. No sense in you hauling me all the way into town and spending half the day when you can patch me up here. For that matter, I can patch myself up."

"Tough girl," Clay muttered again. He stood and scooped her up in the process, being careful with her leg and ribs.

Cold air bit into her skin where the denim lay open. The wound stung, that was for sure. And her whole leg throbbed. The slight movement of Clay lifting her made her slightly nauseous.

He put her in the front seat of Chance's truck. "I came on horseback, so I'll meet you there."

"You don't have to stay," Cherry said.

Clay gave her a look that made her heart trip. Lord, he was handsome. Sandy hair, broad shoulders, slim hips, muscles everywhere. He made her yearn. And right then, all she could think about was that kiss they'd shared last week. Under the mistletoe. He'd surprised her. She hadn't seen it coming. And it had rocked her world.

She watched him get on his horse and take off toward the ranch house.

"You know he's crazy about you," Chance said, starting the truck's engine.

Cherry shook her head. "I'm not the right woman for him."

"Sure about that?"

Cherry nodded. "Positive."

THE MINUTE they got in the door of the old ranch house, Hope ambushed them, making Cherry's hobbling trek to the kitchen chair even slower. The yellow Lab sniffed and whined and wanted to know what was wrong with Cherry.

"It's okay, girl. Go lay down. I'm okay."

"I wondered where she was," Clay said, coming in the door right behind them. He took off his hat and gave the dog a scratch on her ears. "You don't usually go anywhere without her." He eased up on Cherry's free side and helped Chance maneuver her onto a kitchen chair.

Just then, a little bundle of puppy energy came barreling into the kitchen, skidding on the worn linoleum floor. Although Cherry's pain level was causing nausea and a sheen of sweat, she couldn't help but smile. The puppy, her most recent stray, looked like a baby Dalmatian, but appeared to be full grown at barely ten pounds. Cherry had named her Joy, because that's what she was—a bundle of Joy who'd landed on her doorstep at Christmastime.

"I left Hope here guarding the puppy."

"Cute pup," Clay said, automatically lifting the little dog when it wanted to jump.

"Some idiot dropped her on the highway by my front gate."

A slight tightening at the corner of his eye was enough to express his feelings on the subject of abandoned animals. Normally people around these parts *brought* Cherry their strays. They didn't just leave them to the mercy of the elements. "Well, then, she's a lucky pup. How about I put them in the other room so Chance can do his doctoring in peace?" He gave the puppy an absent kiss on its tiny black ears, then patted his leg, indicating Hope should follow him.

Cherry tensed, uneasy over him moving so freely through her house. She didn't normally invite company in and it bothered her how embarrassed she was over the rundown state around her. The gold and yellow vinyl flooring was cracked and buckling. The sink was stained beyond the help of bleach and filled with a rubber drainboard and clean dishes since the dishwasher had long since given up the ghost. The refrigerator had a dent in the door but was one of the more decent appliances in the kitchen—along with the stove. Old and dated, it cooked just fine.

All in all, she ought to count her blessings. She had a roof over her head, a fireplace to keep her warm, running water, and a comfortable bed with plenty of quilts. So what if it wasn't *Good Housekeeping* perfect? It kept the rain and snow out.

Besides, her leg, chest, and head were all throbbing at once. Dang it. She didn't have time for injuries. She could feel her heart beating in near panic, knew better than to show that weakness.

"Relax if you can," Chance said, "and let's see what we're working with here."

Between Chance's medical supplies and Cherry's, the doctor was able to do an adequate job of patching her up. The cut on her head wasn't serious and only required a butterfly bandage. Preserving her modesty, Chance shielded her from Clay's view as he lifted her shirt to check her ribs, noting a slight abrasion and a forming bruise.

"Possibly cracked," he said, "but most likely just a bad bruise. It should heal on its own if you take it easy." He'd already cut away the entire leg of her jeans to above her knee, so he sterilized the wound on her calf, numbed the area, applied ten sutures, then gave her a shot of antibiotics and wrapped her leg in gauze.

Cherry could see the concern in Chance's eyes. Casanova's hoof had caught her in the calf, just below the knee. There was a fairly deep gash but no way to know if that muscle was injured or if any ligaments were torn. Time would tell—probably within the next twenty-four hours. It didn't feel broken, though. It hurt like the devil to stand, but she could maneuver if she had to. She knew how to push past pain.

"I don't want you to put any weight on this leg for several days," Chance said, gently securing the gauze with tape. "On the outside, it looks decent. But unless I do X-rays, we won't know what's going on inside."

"I'll let you know if something feels off once I start moving around a bit," she said.

Clay shook his head. "Didn't you hear the doc say to stay off the leg? He didn't say anything about moving around."

"Clay's right, Cherry. Is there someone we can call to give you a hand?" He glanced out the window at the acres of land and livestock. "You won't be out feeding the livestock or horses for at least a week. And that's just my educated guess. Aside from the mobility issues, I don't want any infection in that wound."

Cherry opened her mouth to reply, but Clay beat her to it.

"I'm staying. I'll take care of the chores."

"Clay—"

"You're not in a position to argue right now, Sugar."

She didn't want to cause a scene. She closed her mouth, decided to fight this battle when she and Clay were alone. She'd gotten out of a bad marriage where a man told her what to do and when to do it. She wouldn't stand for another man doing that. Especially one who had no right.

The doctor rested a hand on her shoulder. "Accept the offered help, Cherry. And I'll let the rest of the folks in town know what's what. I'm sure you'll be overrun with willing hands."

"That's not necessary."

"No," Chance said, quietly. "It's not necessary, but it's a fact. You've lived here long enough to know this community pulls together when there's a need." He packed up his supplies and handed the soiled bandages to Clay who pitched them in the trash can. While Clay's back was turned, Chance gently touched her shoulder again, made direct eye contact. "As long as they *know* there's a need."

It almost seemed as though he was speaking with undercurrents. As though he knew her secret. As though the whole town knew her secret. She glanced away, determined to control her emotions. She was reading more into his look than necessary.

"I'm leaving some pain medication," Chance said. "You're going to be sore. I want to know if the soreness is anything other than just that. You know what pain you can tolerate. Don't try to tough it out if it seems more severe than you expect. That's a good indication that we need to look deeper. Let your body tell you what it needs. If your ribs are too painful to manage, call the office and either Kelly or I will come and wrap you up."

"Should you do that now?" Clay asked.

"I don't want to truss her up too much today if we can get by. She's got enough discomfort to deal with."

"I'll be fine," Cherry said.

"I'm sure you will with this one watching over you like a mother hen." He grinned and tipped his head in Clay's direction. "But I want your promise that you'll call me if something doesn't seem right."

She nodded.

"I'll be back with some crutches."

"I think I have some in the barn," she said, feeling bad that he was taking so much time with her when she'd pulled him away from a holiday party.

"I'll drop some by just in case. No sense in you having to dig for them."

She didn't want to argue and advertise her lack of finances. She wasn't destitute. But she was on a tight budget and didn't have extra funds for medical expenses and crutches.

Clay closed the door behind the doctor, then folded his arms and leaned against the counter, his gaze steady on Cherry. He'd discarded his denim jacket, showing off shoulders that tested the seams of his red flannel shirt. The kitchen was small, but it seemed positively claustrophobic with Clay in it. He filled the space with more than just his body. His presence radiated.

He made her nervous—not fearful nervous. Just *aware* nervous.

"Weren't you on your way to Wyatt's house?"

"Was. Got a detour."

"I hate to keep you from your friends."

"They're your friends, too, Cherry."

"I know . . ." She couldn't finish her thought. Yes, the people of this town were her friends in an arm's length sort of way, but she didn't know how to accept that friendship—to *be* a friend in return. Lord. Where had the bossy, leader-of-the-pack, most popular girl in school gone? How had she so thoroughly lost herself? Granted, school days had been many years ago, but still...

"You hungry?" he asked.

Her attention snapped to the present. Could any woman look at Clay Callahan and not be hungry? She doubted that's how he'd meant his question. "I'll nuke something a little later," she said.

Clay sighed and shook his head. "Like it or not, I'm gonna stay here and take care of you."

"I can call my sister," she said.

"Right. Brooke's a city girl. She knows nothing about running a ranch. Besides, she's got kids and a husband to take care of. It wouldn't be fair to ask her to drop everything and come out here when I'm perfectly capable—and willing—to lend a hand."

"How would you know what my sister's capable of? Or anything about my family, for that matter?" Never mind that she'd had no intention of calling Brooke anyway—partly for the reasons he'd stated. The other reasons were more complicated.

"Darlin', your uncle is Ozzie Peyton." He shook his head and grinned. "If there's one thing that old geezer loves to do, it's to brag on his family."

Cherry ducked her head slightly. For a lot of years, she'd avoided her sweet uncle. And Clay calling him a geezer wasn't by any means an insult. The whole town referred to her uncle and his three cronies as the matchmaking geezers. Lloyd Brewer, Vern Tillis, Henry Jenkins, and Ozzie Peyton. They were determined to marry off every single man or woman in the county. Luckily—or unluckily in her case—she'd already been married. And they'd had enough manners to allow her a mourning period since Dell had died.

Little did they know she didn't mourn. Something else that caused her shame.

"Is Sal coming around to help out?" Clay asked, dragging her out of her thoughts. Sal worked the ranch with her—part time. In Cherry's opinion, he was too old to be doing such physical labor, but he insisted on coming out every day and helping her.

"He's over in Billings with his son's family for the holiday. His boy had some surgery and Sal's helping out."

"How long's he been gone?"

"Just a week."

Clay frowned, a muscle jumping in his jaw. "Woman, why don't you ever ask for help?"

"I've been fine. It's not as though it's spring calving season. Things are slow. I can keep the ice out of the watering holes and feed the animals on my own."

He snorted. "If you work sunup to sundown."

"I'm not afraid of hard work."

He sat across from her at the kitchen table, reached for her hand, and rubbed his thumb gently over the calluses on her palm, causing her breath to catch. "I know. You shouldn't have to work so hard, though. Now that I'm here, you can relax."

"You've got your own ranch to run."

"And two able brothers and a whole slew of employees to carry the load."

"Bragger," she said, trying to smile and lighten the mood.

The way he watched her made her nervous. She wasn't used to the wash of hormones that flooded her when Clay Callahan was around. He made her want. And she had no business wanting what she couldn't have. She didn't trust herself or her judgment when it came to men. She was definitely out of practice. It was better—smarter—to keep her distance. To go about the business of her life and keep her emotions and fairytale dreams in check.

"Are we going to talk about that kiss?"

Her stomach jumped so hard it made her dizzy. She wasn't expecting him to bring that up out of nowhere. He had an unfair advantage. She was wounded. She couldn't walk away. She pulled her hand out of his. "I'd rather not."

He cocked a brow. "Never took you for a wimp."

"Because I'm not." Her chin lifted. "Besides, what's to talk about? There was mistletoe. Everyone kisses under the mistletoe."

"Not like we did, they don't."

She felt her cheeks heat and knew darned well he could see the reaction. She'd been in town picking up supplies and had stopped in at Brewer's Saloon for a burger, forgetting it was Thursday night and half the town showed up on Thursday nights to socialize and give the women a break from cooking. There'd been music, laughter…fun. Something Cherry had had too little of in her life. Abbe Callahan, Clay's sister-in-law, had seen her and dragged her right into the back room and the impromptu party. Next thing she'd known, there was mistletoe above her and Clay Callahan beside her.

She took a breath. "Clay, let it go."

"I'd rather not." He gently tossed her own words back at her.

"Why?"

"Because it's taking everything in me right now not to come around this table and kiss you again."

She let the curtain of her hair fall forward, shielding her face. Quietly, she said, "And I'd probably let you and we'd both regret starting something that we can't finish. I have nothing to offer you."

Something in her tone must have gotten through to him. He rose from the chair, moved toward her. Her heart pounded, but she didn't lift her head. Feather-light, he brushed his hand over her hair. "That's where you're wrong, Sugar."

He moved to the stove, grabbed the closest pot, and filled it with water. And just like that, the mood was broken. On to the next thing. She didn't know whether to be glad or sad.

That's where you're wrong, Sugar. The words were a silky caress that sounded more like a threat.

He opened the refrigerator and stared at the contents. "Hmmm," he murmured and shut the door. She watched as he banged around in her small kitchen looking for cooking utensils. A cabinet door came off in his hands. He stared at it as though wondering how it had ended up in his grip. Cherry just sighed. He'd been in her house before. She could only apologize for its shabbiness so much. And right now, she was too tired and sore and distraught to care.

Well, love, I gotta say this one came as a surprise to all of us—me and Henry and Vernon and Lloyd. And I suspect it might have been some of your doing. Ozzie Peyton gazed at the portrait of his late wife, Vanessa. The love of his life, she'd gone to the hereafter some time back. But he still conversed with her, still felt her as if she was right here in the room with him.

A fire crackled in the fireplace, and colored lights twinkled on the Christmas tree in the corner. Seemed silly for an old man with no family to decorate a Christmas tree, but this had been Vanessa's favorite season. They hadn't been blessed with children of their own, but his Vanessa had been a schoolteacher here in Shotgun Ridge, Montana. Had taught nearly every boy and girl—now man and woman—around here. She would have been so pleased to see the growth in the town. The love and the babies.

Ozzie and his buddies—the matchmaking geezers as folks tended to call them—had decided a few years ago that their town was leaning more toward bachelor cowboys than families and had set about to correct that problem. And a right nice job they'd done, even if he did say so himself. He was proud to say they'd successfully matched up eight couples— well, with a couple of them, they'd had a little help, but why quibble?

This latest turn of events, though, had come right smack out of nowhere. That's why he suspected his beautiful wife. He didn't believe in ghosts, but he *did* believe in angels. And his Vanessa was truly an angel. He'd go nose to toe with anybody who dared to disagree.

Who would have thought that prize bull, Casanova, would take it into his ornery head to step on our niece? Hurt her pretty good, love, but don't you worry. Clay Callahan was right there to give her a helping hand—and I suspect that was your doing. How else would he have known to stop by like that? Pretty sneaky, if you ask me. I couldn't have done it better myself! Ozzie grinned and gazed at his journal. Ever since Vanessa had gone on to Heaven, he'd been keeping a log of his thoughts and plans. It soothed him. This was his main means of communicating with her. Vanessa had been his best friend and confidant all of their married life, and why should that stop now? Besides, she clearly had a little pull with the Man upstairs—she'd proven that when little Kimberly Anderson, who'd been trapped in silence after witnessing the death of her father, had spoken right there in the town square on Christmas Eve. The children had seen the angel. So had Ozzie. And he would recognize his Vanessa anywhere.

Still, there was no reason she should have all the fun. After all, he and Lloyd and Henry and Vern had a reputation to uphold.

I know it's Christmastime, and it's the season for miracles. I suspect it's gonna take a miracle to get that sweet niece of ours to trust again. If Wendell hadn't already passed, I'd go knock him in the head, that's for sure. All that drinkin' and leaving the ranch chores to fall on sweet Cherry's shoulders. How was she supposed to keep up? He was a poor excuse for a husband. And I don't like to wish ill on anyone, but I'm hoping he got a demotion to Hades, rather than being promoted up there with you, love. He glanced again at Vanessa's portrait, thought he saw a twinkle pass over her stunning eyes.

He nodded. *You bet. The Man upstairs keeps good tabs on the going's on down here. I knew he'd have the lay of the land where Wendell was concerned. But if you could just speak to him about Cherry and Clay...the boys and I would be much obliged. Love and healing are what we need to make this Christmas in Shotgun Ridge the best ever, you bet.*

CHAPTER 2

*C*herry woke the next morning and remained still for several seconds, taking inventory. It hurt to draw a deep breath and her leg throbbed like a son of a gun. Taking a shower was going to be tricky. Maybe she could wrap her leg in a plastic trash bag. Or perhaps sit in the tub and hang her leg over the side. Just the thought of it made her tired.

She wore a pair of men's style pajamas—loose drawstring bottoms with a button-up top. She'd had to ask Clay to cut her jeans the rest of the way off, otherwise she'd have never gotten out of them. Between the moisture and mud, she'd been shrink-wrapped in denim, despite the entire leg of material Chance had cut away.

She couldn't believe there'd been a man in her house, seeing her half-clothed, cooking for her, taking care of her.

A man who made her heart trip.

The clock on the nightstand said eight a.m. Weak gray daylight filtered through the window. She hadn't slept this late in years, and the livestock needed tending. She couldn't just lay in bed—never mind that's what Clay Callahan would have her do.

Clay. She had no idea if he was still here. The last thing she remembered was taking a pain pill and falling asleep on the sofa. Yet here she was, beneath the quilts all snug in her bed. Alone, thank goodness. And why in the world would that particular thought pop into her head? She was injured, for heaven's sake. And Clay was a gentleman. A really hot, incredibly virile cowboy, but a gentleman none the less.

Not that she was such a great judge of a man's character. She had scars to prove that.

She glanced around for Hope. The yellow Lab usually slept at the foot of the bed, but she was nowhere in sight. Probably herding that little puppy. Cherry should have taken precautions to partition off the house—not that the little rascal could do too much damage anyway.

Slowly, wincing, she eased aside the quilts and swung her legs out of bed. Her bare feet hit the braided rug, but she could feel the cold seeping up from the scuffed wood. Through the window, she could tell it wasn't snowing, but the forecast was for a chilly December week with a chance of more snow by Christmas. The little kids in the area would be thrilled. The ranchers, not so much.

With some difficulty, she scooted to the end of the bed. The bathroom wasn't far, only a few steps. It seemed like a mile. Steadying herself with the bedpost and then the dresser, she hop-stepped to the bathroom, gritting her teeth as the movement jarred her ribs and stung her calf, sending jolts of pain through her entire body.

Moaning, she flicked on the light and automatically reached for the wrench on the vanity to turn on the water.

The wrench was gone.

And right there attached to her cracked and chipped, pink ceramic tile vanity was a shiny chrome faucet with both hot and cold levers. She stared at it for a moment, her chest squeezing. The hot water lever had been missing for years. It was a pain in the butt to use the wrench to turn it on, but she'd made do. Food for the livestock was a much more important expense than hot water levers.

Clay had done this for her. Tears welled in her eyes, and she blinked them away. What was with all this stupid emotion lately?

She didn't know when or how he'd managed to install a new faucet—he'd only been here one night for goodness sake. Wendell hadn't bothered to fix *anything* around the house. She'd asked—then been sorry because it had always resulted in an argument and blame. A fast learner, she'd stopped asking and started to do her own handyman work. Whatever was beyond her skill, she learned. The Internet had tons of videos on just about anything you wanted to accomplish. Of course, it didn't do a lot of good to learn a repair technique if you didn't have the extra funds to fix what needed fixing.

Hope gave a soft woof and came into the bathroom, nuzzling her nose into Cherry's hand, her whole body wagging in happiness. She glanced at the dog, then turned slowly. Clay was leaning against the open bathroom door, holding the wiggling puppy against his shoulder. It was the sweetest, sexiest thing she'd ever seen. His blond hair showed a slight crease where his hat normally sat, indicating he'd already been outdoors. Lord, the man made her weak in the knees.

"Thank you for the faucet."

He shrugged. "No big deal. Grant had an extra one from remodeling the guest house. He brought it by last night. I'm surprised I didn't wake you up with all the banging. I nearly thought better of it."

The Callahan brothers, Ethan, Grant, and Clay were well-known in Shotgun Ridge for their huge ranch and their highly profitable horse breeding operation. "The last thing I remember was falling asleep on the couch."

"Pretty potent pills the doc left." He reached to the side and brought out a pair of aluminum crutches. "Speaking of Chance, he dropped these by for you. We'll probably need to adjust them, but at least you won't have to hop."

Good Lord. All these visitors and she hadn't heard a thing. "I told him he didn't have to do that. I'm sure I've got a pair in the shed or the barn."

"Well, now you have two. If we run across your set, we'll donate them back to the clinic." He straightened, seemed a little unsure all of a sudden. "Um, do you need any help in here?"

Her mouth opened, but no words came out. She was leaning heavily on the sink and she had no idea how she would accomplish her morning rituals, but the thought of Clay *helping* her turned her insides to jelly.

She wasn't sure she had the strength to tackle the shower yet and decided she'd make do with a washcloth and a bar of soap. Later, she'd figure out how to rig a trash bag to keep her wound water-tight. Right now, though, she didn't have the energy. And every cell in her body was throbbing.

"Um, I think I'm good for now."

He set the puppy on the floor and instructed Hope to herd her in the opposite direction. Well-trained, the Lab did as instructed. Satisfied that the animals weren't underfoot, he stepped into the small, tiled room and propped one of the crutches beside Cherry, measuring the other one to her body.

"Slip this under your arm." Checking the length, he adjusted first one, then the other. "Try that."

She shifted and winced when her weight landed on her injured leg before she could find her balance. Clay's hand shot out to steady her.

"Easy." With a careful, steadying arm around her ribcage, his fingers dangerously close to the underside of her breast, he gently helped her regain her balance and hovered until both crutches were in place. "Feel okay?"

She nodded. Her body throbbed with pain, yet her heart raced with an entirely different feeling.

He searched her features, lifted his hand, and softly ran his thumb along her cheek, his eyes intense on hers. "You're in a lot of pain. I'll get you something to eat so you can take a pill."

It took a moment for her to find her breath. He stood so close she could hardly think. Rather than try to speak, she just nodded again.

He left the bathroom, and she wasn't sure how to feel. She ought to object to him waiting on her. But she simply couldn't find the energy. Pain was an understatement. Her body felt wrecked.

She grabbed a washcloth from beneath the sink, washed as best as she could and brushed her teeth and hair. Just the small amount of grooming wore her out. She almost hobbled back to bed but heard sounds and smells of cooking coming from the kitchen. Originally a Texas girl, her Southern manners kicked in. One didn't stay in bed when company was in the house.

The crutches were more nuisance than help. She ran into the dresser and the wall, put her foot down and suffered a stinging jolt clear up her body, tried hopping, wanted to cry, then finally made it to the sofa where she leaned against the worn arm of the nubby brown fabric, breathing heavily.

She didn't hear Clay come up behind her. The next thing she knew, he'd scooped her into his arms. The crutches fell to the floor, and she gasped.

"Looks like you need a little practice on those sticks."

Her heart was beating triple time. "Practice I won't get if you insist on carting me around."

He lowered her to a chair at the kitchen table, brushed a soft kiss to the bandage at her forehead and grinned. "Call me impatient. The eggs would have turned to rubber by the time you made it to the kitchen."

She shook her head, held on to her smile. The man was incorrigible. And did he need to go around kissing her like that? Oh, it was platonic enough. But tell that to her insides.

Hope came into the kitchen, tail wagging and perched herself next to Cherry. The puppy was nowhere to be seen. Probably not a good thing. Clay grabbed a potholder and slid a perfectly formed omelet from the skillet to a plate, opened the microwave and retrieved several strips of bacon, then pushed the lever down on the toaster, only to stare at it when it popped right back up.

"Toaster's broken."

He glanced at her, perplexed. "Then why keep it out on the counter?"

She shrugged. "I don't know. I just never got around to putting it away. I watched a video on toaster repairs but haven't had a chance to see if it can be fixed."

"How long's it been broke?"

Over a year. "A while."

He pulled the bread from the useless slots, set them on the side of her plate and retrieved butter and jam from the fridge.

She watched him move around the kitchen. He was as at home in this room as he was in the barn or stable. He cleaned as he went, running the sponge over the countertop as though polishing high-gloss granite instead of chipped laminate. Cherry was a fairly neat person. Every once in a while though, she left dishes in the sink or a pan on the stove—because she *could.* It was childish—defiant. But it made her feel powerful.

He set the plate in front of her along with a glass of orange juice and the small white pill that packed such a punch. Hope came to attention, sniffing hopefully at the scent wafting in the air.

"Thank you. I really am uncomfortable with you waiting on me, though."

"That's okay. I'm uncomfortable with you being in pain—so we're even."

Hardly. But she didn't know how to argue with his non-logic. She picked up her fork, tasted the omelet, and realized that she was indeed hungry. He'd added cheese, onions, and spinach. She had no idea where the last ingredient had come from. Certainly not her fridge.

"Did you go to the store? Or do we have grocery delivery now?" she asked.

"Abbe knows I like to cook, so between the main house and the guest house, she keeps the pantry pretty stocked—just in case I decide to take the chore off her hands. She dropped some things off this morning."

"My gosh. How many visitors did I sleep through?"

"Just Grant, Chance, then Abbe."

"You said Abbe keeps the guest house stocked. Are you living there now?" she asked. The three Callahan brothers owned a large, multi-million-dollar horse breeding ranch. Ethan Callahan and his wife Dora and their kids lived in the original family home. Grant and Clay had built another show-stopper of a home on the property as well as a guest house. When Abbe had come to town—on the run from the Las Vegas Mob—she had stayed in their guest house. Now Abbe and Grant were married and living in the main home.

"Yes. I figured Grant and Abbe needed their privacy."

"That's a pretty big house you lived in. Seems there'd be enough room for five families to have privacy."

He grinned. "Yeah, but you know newlyweds. Never knew when I'd open a door and interrupt something. Then the new baby came along and it got pretty noisy. Just makes it easier to hang my hat in the guest house. It's plenty big enough for me...for now."

"You have something against babies?" she asked.

"Not a thing."

She didn't ask him about his last statement—*for now*. She knew he wanted a relationship with her. But she wasn't the right woman for him. And ridiculously, it hurt to think about him falling in love with another woman and needing a bigger home. Because surely Clay Callahan would want the sound of children's voices ringing in the halls of his own home. He would want a woman who didn't come with baggage, who could give him those children.

That woman wasn't her.

Her appetite dwindled halfway through the meal.

"You cooked way too much. Want the rest?" She pushed the plate away, and he sat across from her, accepting the food and her fork. Hope shifted her position and her attention to him.

Somehow, using the same fork made the act of eating more intimate.

He pointed at her juice. "Take the pill."

"It'll put me back to sleep."

"Not that you have anything pressing on your schedule today."

"I really want to try to move around. See if I can work out some of the soreness."

He polished off the rest of the omelet. "Not today."

His matter-of-fact tone hit her the wrong way. Her chest tightened. "I don't need someone telling me what I can and cannot do—today or any day."

His hand paused with a slice of bacon halfway to his mouth. Slowly, he set the food on the plate, leaned forward.

She held her breath. Silence stretched out in the room. *Breathe*, she coached herself, even as the air froze in her lungs.

"Are you afraid of me?" he asked quietly, a frown creasing his handsome face.

She glanced away. "No."

Scooting his chair next to hers, he encouraged her gaze to return to his with a feather-light touch against her cheek. "Look here, Sugar."

She finally met his hazel eyes.

"I don't know the details, but I've got a fairly good idea the asshole you were married to didn't treat you well."

Shame hit her. It was one thing for her to call up the memories. To have someone else—especially Clay—suspect, was nearly intolerable. "All marriages have their ups and downs."

He fingered the ends of her hair that fell past her shoulder, his touch raising the nerve endings on her bare arm. "Dell had a mean streak. Had it when we were kids." Dell had grown up in Shotgun Ridge, so no one was surprised when he decided to return after he'd spent a few years running the rodeo circuit. Maybe a few had been surprised that he'd brought Cherry with him.

"He's gone now, so it doesn't matter."

"True. But he left behind some scars, didn't he?"

"Clay..."

His gaze begged her for honesty. "It's just you and me here, Sugar."

She sighed, pulled away to create a little distance. "Maybe he did."

"And how did I just remind you of him?"

She wasn't used to someone being so astute. "I didn't say—"

"You didn't have to. I triggered you. I want to know how."

She shrugged. "I've gotten used to not answering to anyone. No one telling me what to do."

"I wasn't trying to tell you what to do. I was suggesting. You're hurt and I want to take care of you."

"Well, sometimes, taking care can turn into controlling."

"Not my intention."

"I probably overreacted." She sighed, wanting to steer them from this conversation. "I *am* in a fair amount of pain. And I don't like it. I don't like feeling helpless."

With one fingertip, he pushed the white pill a little closer. "No one does. But I'm a good cook, and I'm excellent with the livestock and pets." He dropped his hand and gave Hope's ears a scratch. The dog—waiting hopefully in case a stray strip of bacon should find its way onto the floor—grinned her approval of his touch. "And it just so happens that my work-load at the ranch is light this time of year. So, why don't you relax and take me up on my offer of help?"

Relax wasn't even in her vocabulary. She thrived on hard work—and was good at it. But the throbbing in her leg won out. She reached for the pill. Never in her wildest dreams had she imagined an incredibly sexy cowboy would be sitting at her kitchen table, offering to take on her responsibilities and cater to her every whim.

It scared her and excited her at the same time.

CHAPTER 3

*V*oices pulled Cherry out of a pain pill-induced sleep. She sat up on the couch, ran her fingers through her hair and pulled the afghan more snuggly around her. From the sound of it, Wyatt and Hannah Malone were in her kitchen, moving toward her front room. A fire was crackling in the fireplace, warming the small space. Clay's doing, of course. Vulnerability stole over her at the thought of him watching her sleep.

"Hey partner," Wyatt said, coming into the room, Hannah and Clay right behind him. "Came by to check on you—and Casanova," he admitted. Last year, she'd sold part interest of her beloved bull to Wyatt so he could start his own registered herd. It had nearly killed her to do so, but she'd been backed into a corner financially. Dell's drinking had impacted every aspect of their ranching operation and his ego had prevented her from taking the reins. They'd waited too long to act and had gotten behind a snowball of debt and two bad seasons at market.

"I'm okay. Everyone's making a bigger fuss than is necessary."

Clay snorted. Wyatt smiled and shook his head.

Hannah eased up next to Cherry on the sofa and took inventory with her eyes. "I told Wyatt we didn't need to bother you so soon, but all he can think about is that bull hurting you. How are you?"

Hannah and Cherry had had a rocky start to their friendship when Hannah had come to Shotgun Ridge after answering a mail-order-bride advertisement for Wyatt—an advertisement that Wyatt knew nothing about. Cherry's Uncle Ozzie and his three geriatric friends had gotten it into their heads that the town was dying with too many bachelors and not enough women and babies, so they'd started a clandestine matchmaking service. Recently, the Bagley widows had joined them in their efforts.

But Cherry had been cautious of Hannah in the beginning. A lot of people thought Cherry had a crush on Wyatt Malone. Oh, she'd thought about what it would have been like if she'd been with a man like Wyatt instead of her late husband, Dell. But that's as far as she'd let herself go. When Hannah had shown up, Cherry had felt protective over Wyatt—because he was a friend and he'd been grieving the loss of his wife and son. Her own grief wasn't the same as Wyatt's, but she certainly understood devastation. So, she'd kept an eye out—which had possibly given the town's folk the wrong impression.

But Hannah, with her sweet disposition and total ineptitude for anything to do with ranch life, hadn't allowed Cherry's aloofness to deter her from forming a friendship.

"I'm okay. Just sore and bored and mad that I can't get up and tend to my own business."

Hannah smiled. "Well, you have plenty of willing help, so take advantage. Besides, it's getting cold out there and a good book by the fire is not such a bad way to spend the day."

"If I could keep my eyes open long enough to read. Clay keeps pushing those pain pills on me, and the next thing I know, five hours have passed without me knowing it."

Wyatt sat across from her in the recliner chair, and Clay tossed another log on the fire.

"So, what happened?" Wyatt asked. "Should we worry about Casanova's disposition?"

"No." Cherry shook her head, understanding his worry, even though it gave her a twinge of annoyance and made her feel defensive and protective over Casanova. The bloodlines in a registered herd needed to be pure—and that included the emotional makeup of the animal as well as the physical. "It wasn't his fault. Something could have bitten him. Maybe he was stung by a bee. I was laying out the salt lick and wasn't paying attention. He's never objected to me being close to him at all. Something spooked him. That's all. Dumb, stupid mistake on my part for not standing clear."

Clay snorted and gave the fire another poke. She ignored him. She was well aware of his opinion of her and the bull. He thought she treated Casanova like a pet. And maybe she did. But that bull was hers—or had been until she'd had to sell a part of him to Wyatt. Casanova had been a wedding gift from her parents, a dowry that had the potential to ensure the health of her financial future. The problem was, Wendell hadn't pulled his weight when it came to the ranch. And there was only so much Cherry had been able to accomplish on her own. Or had been *allowed* to accomplish.

"Mind if I ask Lyle Watkins to come out and have a look?"

Her first instinct was to say no. Lyle Watkins was Dora

Callahan's brother who'd recently moved to Shotgun Ridge and taken over the town's veterinary practice. She couldn't afford a vet bill. But she wasn't going to advertise that in a room full of her neighbors. Never mind that Lyle came from oil money and quite often chose not to charge his clients.

"I don't think it's necessary, but if it'll make you feel better to have *your* half of the bull looked at, be my guest." She smiled, hoping her words came across as light-hearted teasing.

Wyatt winked at her. "Lyle owes me a favor, so I'll give him a call. Just wanted to get your go-ahead before I invite others onto your property. Don't want you shooting the cavalry for trespassers."

"I'll keep the safety on the shotgun."

Hannah reached for her hand. "What can we do for you before we go? I know you're tired and need to rest."

"I'm set," Cherry said. "Clay's insisting on cooking and taking over the chores. I can't think of anything else I need at the moment."

Hannah stood, and so did Wyatt. "Well, if you think of anything, you know we're right next door." If more than a mile could be considered right next door.

Clay walked Wyatt and Hannah to the door. Cherry took the opportunity to hobble to the bathroom, giving her crutches another trial run. She was athletic—ranching life ensured that—so she managed fairly well. Needing to move around a bit, she clumped her way to the kitchen and grabbed the tea kettle, intending to heat some water for coffee. She needed caffeine to shake off the grogginess of the pain medication.

"Sit," Clay ordered, coming up behind her.

"I believe we've already discussed your bossiness and my dislike for it."

"Sorry. All these years living with my brothers have obviously eroded my good manners. Please sit down, Sugar, and let me wait on you. What was it you were after?"

She rolled her eyes. "Coffee."

"From a tea kettle?" He gently herded her toward a kitchen chair. "Not on my watch."

She smelled the rich aroma of coffee beans as he opened a bag sitting on the counter. Next thing she knew, a machine she'd never before seen sitting on her poor old scarred countertop was whirring and grinding and gurgling, filling the room with the most divine fragrance.

"Where did that come from?" She held up her hand. "Never mind. I can guess. Another delivery from someone in your family?"

"Abbe. Brought it this morning with the groceries. I hadn't taken the time to set it up yet."

"Nothing wrong with instant."

He raised a brow, set a steaming cup in front of her. "Say that after you've tasted."

Her taste buds did an incredibly happy dance. She hated to agree with him. He was entirely too smug. But, goodness, this was heavenly. "Okay, you win this round."

"Of course, I do. I'm excellent in all things kitchen related."

She smiled. "Who taught you kitchen skills?"

"My dad. Taught all of us, actually—Grant and Ethan and me. Grant and Ethan are both good cooks—but mainly for survival purposes. And God help us when Dora gets in the kitchen. Makes me shudder."

"She can't cook?"

"Oh, she can cook. It's her method that drives me nuts.

She's like a little whirlwind and she's super disorganized and messy."

"But she gets the job done and her family doesn't go hungry."

"True. But for a neat-nick like me, it's a bit stress-inducing." He gave the countertop a quick swipe with the towel, then joined her at the table with his own cup. "I thought about being a chef at one time. But decided I was needed more in the family horse business than a restaurant."

"I don't think I could picture you running Brewer's Saloon."

"I'll have you know I've helped out a time or two when they were short-staffed. Especially when Becky and Timmy died."

"Oh, that was sweet of you." Becky and Timmy were Wyatt Malone's late wife and child. They were also Iris and Lloyd Brewer's daughter and grandson. When they'd died in a car accident, the whole town had grieved. Not only had Wyatt needed help, so had Iris and Lloyd with their restaurant.

Clay shrugged. "I was happy to do it, and glad I had the know-how."

He had quite a few skills, she thought. The Callahan and Sons ranch ran like a well-oiled machine. Clay had a hand in every facet of the operation but handled the racing end of the business almost exclusively. He could cook, take care of injured women and stray puppies, keep order among the livestock, and repair hot water levers on old faucets. If she wasn't careful, she might find herself relying on him too much. Or falling for him.

She took another sip of the excellent coffee, then nearly spilled it when someone knocked on the door. She'd never, in all her years of living in Shotgun Ridge, had this much company in the space of two days. Not that her neighbors weren't friendly. But Wendell hadn't encouraged friendships. And after he'd died, Cherry hadn't known how to change the aloneness and aloofness she'd learned to perfect so well, the walls she'd erected to hide behind.

She automatically reached for her crutches.

"Stay put." He stopped, paused. "I mean, don't get up." He stopped again, raked his hand through his hair. "Honest to God, I'm not being bossy. It's just...is it okay if I answer the door?"

She bit her bottom lip to hold in a smile. He was so frustrated, and so cute about it. Clearly not used to thinking about his words before he spoke. The fact that he did so, that he'd listened to her, *heard* her, made her insides melt. Made her wonder if trusting a man might actually be a possibility.

"Yes, please don't keep whoever's there standing out in the cold."

Normally people felt free to walk into their neighbors' kitchens with a perfunctory knock and a shout. Cherry's kitchen was an exception.

Clay's brother Ethan and sister-in-law Dora came in.

"Oh, you poor thing," Dora said, setting a plate of decorated Christmas cookies on the dinette table. "How are you feeling?"

"A little overwhelmed, I think."

Dora laughed. "Not used to all of us, hmmm? Is Clay taking good care of you?"

"I think so. I've been sleeping most of the day, so I can't say for sure."

"I am wounded," Clay said. "Of course, I'm taking excellent care of her—when she lets me."

Hope came trotting into the kitchen with the puppy

jumping at her hind legs. "Oh! A baby Dalmatian," Dora exclaimed. She snatched her camera out of the satchel she still had slung over her shoulder and started taking shots.

"That's Joy. My latest stray. And she's not a Dalmatian. When I found her, she was full of mats, so I shaved her and this is what was under all the hair. I suspect she's more spaniel or Maltese, maybe." Cherry knew Dora's love of photographing baby animals. The other woman had been known to come knocking on the neighbors' doors scouting out new subjects to capture through her Nikon's viewfinder. She sold the photos to greeting card companies. Not that she needed the money. Dora's grandfather was a Texas oilman who'd left his granddaughter and her four brothers a trust fund about the size of Montana. Plus, Ethan—along with *his* brothers—had more money than God with their successful horse breeding farm.

Cherry wasn't sure why her mind automatically gravitated to the size of the Callahan's bank accounts. She in no way begrudged any of them their good fortune, and she wasn't intimidated by them. But it made her hyper-aware of her own surroundings—of her discomfort and shame. Silly that she couldn't get past it. Her neighbors didn't judge her. But she judged herself. This wasn't the life she'd envisioned for herself. She wasn't the person she'd envisioned being. And she just wasn't sure how to change things. She hated feeling mistrustful. Hated that it was so easy to push one of her many fearful hot buttons. Wondered why, when the need for control was so strong within her, she'd so completely surrendered it to Dell. Wondered if she'd ever climb out of the anger and shame she felt—directed at herself.

She saw Dora lower the camera, then move toward the doorway to peek into the front room. Normally, visitors were polite enough to wait for an invitation to move through someone's house—Clay excluded, of course. But Dora was like a mini-whirlwind. She talked and moved so quickly, it was hard to keep up. Cherry ran a mental visual of the living room where crochet afghans were draped across the sofa and recliner. Cattle magazines and livestock breeding manuals littered the coffee table, but otherwise, the room was spare and clean.

"Where is your Christmas tree?" Dora asked, snapping one more shot of the puppy frolicking around the ever-patient Lab.

"I don't usually put one up," Cherry said. "It's just me, so..." Her words trailed off at the horrified look on Dora's face.

"That's awful. How do you get in the spirit without all the decorations and stuff? My goodness, it's already the first of December. We can't have this! Clay, you'll see to it, won't you?" she demanded of her brother-in-law.

"That's not—" Cherry never got the chance to finish her sentence.

"On second thought—Ethan, you go get her a tree," she ordered her husband. "Clay's got other things to do for now. I'll come back with the kids and we'll get it looking more like Christmas in here."

"That's not—" Again, she didn't get a chance to complete her sentence.

"Of course, it's necessary," Dora finished for her, then raised her camera and clicked several times as Joy came prancing into the room carrying a black shoelace in her mouth. Someone would need to investigate the shoe that lace had come from.

Cherry scooped up the puppy and dropped an automatic kiss to the soft fur of Joy's ears.

"Might as well not argue," Ethan said with an indulgent smile in his wife's direction. The love shining in his eyes was nearly blinding.

"I promise we'll keep all the kids corralled and you won't have to do a thing but rest on the sofa. Oh, they're going to have so much fun—the kids, that is." Dora reached down and trailed a hand over Cherry's shoulders, then gave a quick scratch under Joy's chin. She was a toucher. Something Cherry wasn't used to...or totally comfortable with. But there was little to do in the wake of Dora's bulldozer personality.

And the idea of having children in her house was a draw she didn't want to put too much emphasis on.

~

WHEN DORA CALLAHAN HAD AN AGENDA, she didn't mess around. Later that evening, the neighbors came bearing food, wine, baked goods, and Christmas decorations. The pine walls of Cherry's living room were bursting at the seams with children and adults. Christmas music played from a Bluetooth speaker Ethan had brought—along with the six-foot balsam fir. The smell of popcorn and evergreen filled the air. It made Cherry feel giddy. She hadn't smelled these smells or experienced this Christmas spirit since she'd left her hometown in Texas more than five years ago.

Clay had dragged some decorations out of Cherry's attic, and the rest of the neighbors had arrived carrying a box of their own. The children strung popcorn and made paper garlands, supervised by Opal and Mildred Bagley. The widows—sisters who'd married brothers—lived in town and had turned their white two-story home on Main Street into a boarding house. The antics and bickering of the two ladies was entertainment all by itself. Cherry had heard rumors that the widows were horning in on her uncle's matchmaking endeavors.

Almost as though she'd conjured him with her thoughts, Uncle Ozzie came and sat next to her on the sofa. "How's my favorite niece?"

"Annoyed. I have a ranch to run and I don't have time to be laid up."

"Now, don't you worry about all the to-dos. Let the rest of us pitch in, you bet."

"That's not so easy for me." All these decorations. As beautiful as they were, right now, all she could think about was having to put them away after the season. Her leg would be fully healed by then, so there wouldn't be a need for the neighbors to swarm. It would just be her again. On her own.

"I know," Ozzie said, his shrewd, vivid blue eyes studying her, seeing more than she wanted him to. "Never been one to reach out to folks. Have a feeling that was Dell's doing. I hold myself responsible for not stepping in. Always had an inkling things weren't up to snuff where that boy was concerned."

Cherry looked away. Her worst nightmare was people actually *knowing* the truth—exactly what kind of man Dell had really been.

When Dell had insisted on moving to Shotgun Ridge, Cherry had agreed, thinking it would be a fresh start for them, give Dell the purpose he'd lost when he'd had to retire from the rodeo circuit. And the fact that her uncle lived here and had offered a helping hand had been a bonus.

Or so she'd thought.

She hadn't dreamed she'd end up retreating from everyone she cared about.

"It was fine. Nothing anybody could do about his drinking."

"So you always said." Obviously sensing her discomfort—and understanding the time and place wasn't right for this type of conversation—Ozzie changed the subject.

"Got a lot planned this season. Emily Bodine's running wild with the live nativity over at the church again this year. Expecting quite a crowd, you bet. I imagine she'll be around signing you up for a part."

Cherry smiled at her uncle. His tendency to tack on *you bet* to nearly all his sentences was endearing. He always tried to involve her in the town's doings. And she always resisted—unless it had to do with work. Looking at all of the happy people in her living room, she felt something begin to melt inside her. Especially when she looked at Clay. Maybe this year she wouldn't resist so hard.

"I guess I could watch over the cattle or something."

"Long as they don't step on you, you bet." Ozzie gave a chuckle and gently patted her knee.

"Ozzie Peyton!" Opal Bagley declared, clearly eavesdropping. "What a thing to say. Here that sweet girl has her leg all wrapped up from that very occurrence and you go projecting more injuries onto her!"

"I'm sure he wasn't *projecting*, Sister," Mildred said with a sniff, patting Ozzie on the shoulder. "Still, cattle are so unpredictable. I think we'll make better use of Cherry's time with us at the hot chocolate booth. Plenty of soft chairs so she can rest her poor leg."

"I'm sure my 'poor leg' will be fine in time for the nativity production." Although tonight it was throbbing pretty good and didn't feel like it would be better any time in the foreseeable future.

"Oh, splendid!" Opal crowed, directing a quick wink at Ozzie. "So, we'll count on you. Hear that, Sister? She's coming to the production this year."

Cherry opened her mouth to object, then closed it. She'd been had by three geriatric meddlers.

Clay, watching her from the corner, passed the baby he was holding to Stony Stratton and moved toward her. She'd noticed that the fathers in the room—Ethan, Grant, and Stony —were caring for the babies while their wives corralled the toddlers and young ones, assisting them in decorating the tree. Nikki Stratton and Ian Malone were the oldest of the children, and the most intent on the job at hand—until the puppy caught their eye. Then they were momentarily distracted, giving Hannah and Eden and Dora time to rearrange the ornaments clumped too close together without offending a little one.

Cherry drank in every detail of the activity happening around her, including the sexy stride of the cowboy moving toward her. Goodness, he made her heart trip.

Clay took Ozzie's vacated place beside her on the couch and crossed a booted ankle over his knee. "No getting out of it now, Sugar." He smelled of Christmas tree, crisp night air, and pure man. It took everything within her not to lean in and inhale.

"Who said I'm trying to get out of it?"

He winked and tucked a strand of hair behind her ear. "I know you."

Her heart melted a little more. She wasn't sure if the response was to his claim to *know* her, or his touch. Probably both.

Once the lighted angel rested in the place of honor at the top of the tree, placed there by Grant—the tallest of the

Callahan brothers—Ozzie plugged in the lights. Strands of colored bulbs twinkled like candy-colored fireflies among the fragrant branches of the fir, blinking against the various shaped glass balls and paper chain links. Cherry wanted a closer look, wanted to reminisce, but decided to wait until later when she wouldn't take the chance of losing her balance in front of her friends. Some of the ornaments were new to her, some handmade, but some were her own and carried a lifetime of memories. She could see the red felt reindeers and the Cinderella horse and carriage she'd cherished since childhood.

Eden Stratton pulled out her guitar and strummed a few chords of "Jingle Bells". The kids broke out in song. Cherry could hear Clay's soft baritone as he joined in. A lot of giggling ensued as the kids changed the lyrics, and the next thing Cherry knew, childish voices—Nikki and Ian's--were singing at the tops of their lungs about superheroes' poor hygiene and Santa losing his sleigh. Nikki Stratton switched songs mid-lyric and shouted out that Grandma got run over by a reindeer."

Cherry was so tickled she burst out laughing.

Clay went absolutely still. He loved seeing Cherry this way. Didn't think he'd *ever* seen her so open, with her guard relaxed. She was gorgeous. Beautiful, creamy skin. Vivid blue eyes. Her red hair shining and hanging past her shoulders, wispy bangs brushing her red eyebrows. She looked like she belonged on the cover of a magazine. She wore a perfectly respectable pair of pajama pants to accommodate her bandaged leg, and an open zippered hooded sweatshirt over a form-fitting thermal shirt. She'd been horrified at her state of undress—as she'd put it—when the neighbors had shown up. But Clay thought she looked fine. In fact, he'd

see why I should want to be with mine. My place was here with him. So, we didn't celebrate."

"Your family was okay with that?"

"What could they do? I made excuses for why we couldn't come home. And I made excuses why Mom and Dad couldn't visit. It was just easier once Dell started drinking. When he drank, he wasn't super pleasant to be around."

"He isolated you."

She shrugged. "You can't put all the blame on him. I let him."

He pushed back a lock of her hair. "That's a conversation you're not going to win with me, Sugar."

"It's true. No one can *make* you do anything," she said, repeating something she'd believed all her life.

"No?"

His gaze was strong and steady. He saw so much. And that made her feel vulnerable, yet oddly safe at the same time. She wasn't sure why she was so determined to take on all the blame for her life. But how could she tell anyone that Wendell had abused her and she hadn't left him? That was on her, wasn't it? Her parents would have helped her leave him. Uncle Ozzie would have, for sure. She didn't want to get into that now. Not with Clay. She couldn't bear to look any weaker in his eyes.

So, she changed the subject. "I wish you hadn't asked Ethan to take the horses to your place."

"It's just for a while. You've got so many little critters around here to take care of, seemed the boarded horses could rest their haunches in a different stall for a week or two."

"We should have checked with the owner's first—"

"Already done."

"And how did you know who they belonged to?"

"Sugar, you've got records more organized that I do with names on stalls and tack labeled and emergency phone numbers. Easy enough. And as soon as I explained about your injury, every single owner was ready to hitch up their trailers and come move the horses themselves. People care about you, Cherry."

"I hardly know my boarding clients." The town was growing rapidly since her uncle had gone on a matchmaking campaign to fill it with women and children. New people were moving here daily, wanting a slice of peace and community spirit and wide-open spaces. The horses she boarded were for families new to the area who hadn't yet gotten their homes and barns completed. It worked out well for Cherry. She had the room and needed the money. Win-win.

A log in the fireplace popped. Clay studied her for a moment. "Why is it so hard for you to accept help? You're always one of the first to show up when folks need a hand rounding up stray cattle or rebuilding a barn."

"That's work. I'm capable. No sense in letting my skills go to waste. I'm good with animals and problem-solving. Not so great with people skills."

"You did okay tonight."

She smiled. "Yeah. I guess I did. Dora's hard to resist. It's just…"

"Just what?" He brushed her bangs from her forehead, trailed his fingers lightly over the bandage at her temple.

"I'm not sure if I remember how to be social for longer than a few hours. I think I've forgotten."

"Dell helped you forget, I imagine." His jaw tightened. "I'd like a chance to take a poke at him."

She didn't bother to admonish him over speaking ill of the dead. If she were honest, she'd like to take a swing at Dell, too. She'd like a do-over—one in which she had some of her old fire and courage, where she didn't take any guff from anyone.

He leaned in closer. Firelight danced over his skin, highlighting the slight stubble on his jaw.

He was so close. Would he kiss her? Should she let him?

"What do you want for Christmas?" The whispered words caressed her face.

You. She didn't dare voice that thought. She shrugged.

"Ask me what I want." His voice was still soft, his eyes unwavering.

"Clay...no."

"Then I'll tell you. I want *you.* In my stocking." His lips barely brushed the bandage at her temple. His warm breath traveled across her face, her lips.

She wanted to repeat that kiss they'd shared under the mistletoe at Brewer's Saloon. Badly.

Instead, she pulled back. "This isn't a good idea."

"Too fast?"

"This isn't a thing, Clay."

"Felt like a thing to me when we were at Brewer's. Why'd you run?"

Her heart was beating so hard she felt a little dizzy. "I'm not running."

"Only because you can't." He gently caressed her calf, skimming his fingers over the raised edges of the bandage through the soft cotton of her sweatpants. "Makes me feel like I'm taking advantage."

"Maybe you are."

"Do you honestly feel that way?"

She sighed. "No. But we've got no business repeating that kiss. There's no future there."

"You really believe that? I could prove you wrong in two seconds flat."

She stiffened. He misread her reaction. "Aw, Sugar. I did it again, didn't I?"

His voice was so tender, so understanding, she wanted to cry. And she wasn't a woman to cry. Why couldn't she have met him when she'd been carefree and full of life and fun? Before she'd learned to guard every thought, emotion and word? When she was still capable of giving a man her trust.

CHAPTER 4

During the three days since her accident, Clay had worked from sunup to sundown caring for her entire ranch—and for her. He made her feel cherished. Valued. More, even, that she didn't want to name.

Cherry watched him through the kitchen window, the late morning light sparkling through the glass. He wore another of the red flannel shirts he seemed to favor, along with his sheepskin-lined denim jacket, jeans and white Stetson. White hat. Yes, he was definitely one of the good guys.

He'd erected a puppy pen for Joy to keep her corralled while he was outdoors, and had stooped to offer her some sort of treat which caused the puppy to dance on her hind legs. Clearly, he was working on teaching her some nice dog manners to go with her adorableness.

Just then, a white truck with a boom lift pulled up the lane. It had the dark green Callahan and Sons logo on the door and Grant was at the wheel. Determined to have the outdoors of her ranch sparkling as brightly and Christmassy as the indoors, Clay had obviously enlisted his brother's help in stringing Christmas lights. For a minute, she felt a twinge of discomfort. The exterior of both the house and barn weren't in the best of shape. Stringing lights would give the Callahan brothers an up close and personal inspection of the lack of maintenance.

Nothing she could do about it now. Grant was already getting out of the truck and hauling boxes of Christmas lights with him. Where in the world did they store all of this stuff? Silly question. The Callahans had more property and outbuildings than anyone in the county. She saw Grant lean over and scratch Joy's ears. The puppy danced on her hind legs again, her little ears flopping as she nearly jumped over the makeshift pen. Hope stood by, patiently waiting for the puppy to settle so she could scoop up a belly rub from the new arrival.

This was another thing she appreciated about Clay. Puppies required a lot of work and attention and energy. Clay had completely taken over, not only her large animals, but her pets, too, making sure they were fed and entertained and that they didn't jump on her injuries or require her to caretake in any way. Even though it was hard to let him run her show, his babysitting Joy and Hope had been an absolute blessing. It made her wonder how in the world the new mothers in town found the strength to care for their helpless little babies when they got sick.

She pretty much answered her own question. They had doting husbands. They were part of a loving team, and that clearly made all the difference.

She and Clay were becoming somewhat of a team. Temporarily, of course. But the way he doted on those dogs simply melted her heart.

Cherry's cell phone rang, pulling her away from the sweet scene. Caller ID showed it was her mom.

"How you doing, hon?" Joanne Peyton asked as soon as Cherry answered.

Uh-oh. She knows. "Hey, Mama. I'm doing okay."

"That's not what I heard," Joanne said tentatively.

Cherry sighed. "Uncle Ozzie called, didn't he?"

"Well, if he didn't, we'd never know what's going on with you. What in the world happened? And did you have X-rays? I know how stubborn you can be."

She gave her mom an edited version of the accident. No sense admitting she'd been knocked out and still had trouble drawing a deep breath.

"So, your Uncle Ozzie says the neighbors are pitching in to help you out. You know Daddy and I can hop on a plane if you need us."

"No, Mama. That's not necessary. I'm feeling much better today." Only a little fib. "Besides, I know Daddy's busy with the ranch, and you all are getting ready for Christmas."

"Doesn't mean we can't stop and come see about you."

"I really am fine. No broken bones. Just a little cut and bruise on my leg. You know how bruises can hurt worse than anything, but they're not serious."

"You need to get some more help out there for those animals. This wouldn't have happened if you weren't so alone."

"I have Sal, Mama." Never mind that he was away for the holiday. "And Clay Callahan and his brothers have been helping." She didn't dare tell her Clay was basically living with her. She wasn't ready for the kind of questions a revelation like that would bring. She realized she was dancing around and leaving out a whole lot in this conversation. Old habits were difficult to break.

"Have you thought any more about coming home for Christmas?"

"I don't think I'll make it this year, Mama. It's just me with all this livestock."

"I'm sure your neighbors wouldn't mind continuing to fill in."

"That would be asking a lot. It's one thing to accept help for an injury and another completely for hopping on a plane for a vacation."

"Well, then. Daddy and I can hire someone to take care of the animals for a week. It would be so wonderful to see you, hon. Brooke and the kids miss you, too. You won't believe how big those girls of hers are getting. Besides, I can't bear the thought of you being alone at Christmastime."

Mama thought she was grieving. She worried about each 'first' since Dell's death. One day, when Cherry found her feet and figured out what flaw had caused her to stay in a bad marriage, she might sit with Mama and tell her about it.

She didn't see that happening in the foreseeable future.

Cherry did look forward to her weekly phone calls with her mom, though. Mom had started the ritual right after Dell's funeral. During her marriage, communication with her family had dwindled—Cherry's fault. Dell always wanted to eavesdrop on her conversations, then he'd give her the third degree over the tiniest thing she might have said that he had totally misconstrued. If she tried leaving the room to talk in private, he'd accuse her of hiding secrets. So, Cherry had stopped answering the phone, instead sending a quick text when she'd seen the missed calls: *"So sorry I missed your call. I'm right in the middle of*—whatever she made up at the time. *I love you. Talk soon."* She'd hated the lies. But it was better than setting off Dell.

Her parents were busy ranchers, so time seemed to slip by. Months would go by without them actually talking—just quick text messages. Cherry told herself that she *was* keeping in contact. But she was hiding.

"I'll be okay, Mama. The neighbors are determined to keep me busy. But I'll miss you all."

"Well, if you change your mind, hon, you give a holler. Daddy and I will make all the arrangements."

"I love you, Mama. I promise I'll plan a visit soon."

CHERRY SAT on the side of the tub with a heavy black trash bag and a piece of elastic she'd pulled out of a pair of sweatpants. She refused to take any more of those mind-numbing pain pills and had switched to regular ibuprophen. It helped, but not nearly enough. She was tempted to shoot herself up with a nerve block—the kind she kept on hand for emergency C-sections with the cattle.

A poultice—one she also used on the animals—sat next to her on the sink counter. She intended to use it on herself after her shower. She grabbed the sink to leverage herself up and knocked over the hand soap. The dispenser hit the tile floor with a clang.

Clay was at the half-open door in an instant. He paused, taking in her little tank top and tiny lace underwear. The one thing she'd done after Dell died was splurge on sexy undergarments. It was such a frivolous purchase, using money she could ill afford to spend. But something deep in the core of her needed that bit of beauty and femininity beneath her clothes. It gave her a measure of strength that she couldn't explain. Made her feel like the confident woman she'd been once upon a time.

A secret all her own.

After a brief second to take in her state of undress, he moved into the room.

"Need some help with that?"

She started to say no, then paused. Oh, what the heck. He'd already seen her in her underwear. "I thought my engineering skills were fairly good, but I'm not sure if I can actually accomplish this and make it water-tight. And I'm dying to get in the shower and wash my hair." Since the accident, she'd managed to rinse her hair and body in the sink, but it was a huge ordeal.

"Let's see what you've got here." He eased her onto the commode, then sat on the edge of the tub, carefully propping her leg in his lap.

"I thought maybe the elastic would work. I'm having second thoughts. I have duct tape, as well."

"Mmm. I see." He opened both ends of the plastic and slid it over her leg, up to her thigh.

The touch of his fingertips raised goosebumps all over her body. Her heartbeat quickened.

He glanced up, his hazel eyes full of an emotion she didn't dare ponder.

"I think the tape will work better. You'll have to cut it off after your shower, but I imagine it'll keep the water out."

He wrapped the tape above and below her injury, then folded the plastic down and added more tape. Cherry hadn't thought of doing it that way. She would have taped the bag to her skin. And that would have been a nightmare to remove and sent her straight back to bed.

"Thank you," she said shyly.

"Sure thing." Clay left the bathroom to give her some privacy. It was getting more difficult by the day to keep from touching her, kissing her. But he was determined to ease her along, build her trust. Just like with a skittish horse.

Still, he knew he was hovering but couldn't help himself. The damned woman was so independent it was maddening.

A beautiful scent always seemed to emanate from her. Very subtle. He hadn't seen any perfume bottles in the bathroom. Only a simple bottle of lotion on her dresser. He squirted a pump, smelled. Yes, that was it. Cherry blossoms. He wondered if that was deliberate or accidental. Red hair. Cherry name. Cherry scent. Whatever. He loved it. She made him long to taste.

But she wasn't ready for that. He needed to take it slow, establish the intimacy of friendship before he pushed for the intimacy of passion. Whatever Dell had done to her to make her so aloof and mistrustful was still a mystery. Oh, he had his suspicions. But he couldn't spend a lot of time dwelling on those scenarios. It made him too mad. And he'd already figured out that moodiness would definitely send her in the opposite direction.

THE CHRISTMAS SEASON was beautiful in Shotgun Ridge. It was one of Clay's favorite times of the year. And having Cherry beside him in the retrofitted hay wagon, where sleds replaced the wheels, hooked up to a pair of well-behaved horses with jingle bells around their yokes, made it even more special. He wanted to be the man to show her a good time, to give her experiences her jerk of a husband had stolen from her.

Although it had been less than a week since her injury, she was managing well enough and he figured the outing would be good for her.

The air had a sharp bite to it. Snow fell gently, creating a blanket of white that perfected the ambiance of their homey small town. Every year the church put on a drive-through nativity production the first weekend in December, and it seemed as though everyone in town played a part. Wyatt was in charge of the sheep—cattlemen didn't trust the critters not to mow down their prime grazing land, so he considered it his duty to protect his neighbors' land should the sheep get loose. Chance Hammond was normally in charge of the donkeys, but last year, Chance got kicked by one of the more cantankerous of the bunch and they decided he'd better stick to doctoring rather than the animals. This year, he and his wife Kelly were manning the first aid booth. So, minding the donkeys was Clay's job tonight—thus the shepherd costume he wore.

He hadn't donned his headpiece yet. A spark of macho vanity had him wanting to look good for Cherry, and it was tough to look sexy when draped in a belted sheet with long johns underneath. At least he could hang on to his hat for as long as possible.

The night was so clear you could see for miles across the prairie. Christmas lights twinkled in candy colors from every available space across the eaves of the storefronts in town. Carly McCall's boutique windows glittered with festively draped mannequins. Cotton batting strewn with old-fashioned buttons and lace made the storefront window look as though it was covered in freshly-fallen snow.

At the end of Main Street, a twenty-foot Douglas fir, decorated with twinkling lights and huge shiny ornaments straddled the courthouse lawn and the churchyard. A bright shining star rested atop the tree.

"You warm enough?" He adjusted the shared blanket over their knees.

"Yes. It's all so beautiful," she said, a touch of wonder in her normally matter-of-fact tone.

"You didn't come last year, did you?" Clay asked, even though he knew the answer. He'd been yearning for Cherry for so long, he'd always been hyper-aware whenever she showed up to any event.

"No. It's been a while."

"Well, you missed a big show last Christmas. The whole town got to see a true, larger than life miracle."

"I heard about it." Cherry shifted closer to Clay, felt the heat of his thigh against hers as the sled wagon traveled down Main Street, the horse's hooves clopping in the slushy snow. She had lapped up every bit of information she could when the town had been so abuzz over little Kimmy Anderson, who hadn't spoken in months due to a tragedy she'd seen, had begun to talk right there in the town square. She'd claimed an angel had told her it was okay to talk now.

Christmas. The season of miracles where anything is possible.

That's what Ozzie Peyton had declared. Was it really? Could it be for Cherry? Oh, she wished...

Snowflakes drifted softly, settling in the cattleman's crease of Clay's white Stetson. Cars were lined up behind a barricade manned by one of Sheriff Cheyenne Bodine's deputies. It was a huge production—even drawing more people since the sheriff's wife, Emily Bodine, had taken over the marketing of the event.

"This is crazy amazing," Cherry said, craning her neck to get a better look at a knobby-kneed camel resting by the side of the road.

"We had the camels trucked in from a farm over in Billings. They raise them for petting zoo events. Wyatt provided the cows and sheep, and Stony brought the horses."

"Is that Clyde Davis's llama?"

"Yeah. That's Fancy."

Cherry had helped the town rebuild Clyde's barn when it had burned last year. She knew Wyatt had been housing the llama and her young one in his barn for a while.

"This production has grown." Cherry hadn't been to the nativity scene in several years. First, because Wendell didn't want to go. Then because she'd felt like an outsider. She had so many secrets, and she felt like they radiated from her, that the whole town could see her guilt and her shame.

She wasn't sure how Clay had talked her into coming in the first place. Well, actually, it had been Mildred and Opal Bagley who'd sneakily maneuvered her into attending—earlier in the week when they'd come to decorate her tree. Clay had taken it from there and wouldn't let her back out.

"Joy to the World" played through huge speakers positioned on the church steps. A tent with portable heaters housed tables laden with cookies, cakes, hot chocolate, and steaming coffee. That's where Clay deposited her, into the welcoming care of Mildred and Opal Bagley.

He lifted her from the wagon, swinging her into his arms in deference to her injured ribs, and settled her in a plastic folding chair, pulling another chair over to prop up her leg. She was highly uncomfortable with this fussing and attention but didn't know what to do about it.

"Here, now, sweet girl," Opal said. "You just sit right down and rest."

"I can help." She'd never not pulled her weight before and wasn't about to start now—injury or not.

"Of course, you can," Mildred chimed in. "In a minute, when you warm up. Now, Clay, go on with you and mind those donkeys. We'll take good care of our Cherry."

"Yes, ma'am." He grinned and gave a soft peck to Mildred's, and then Opal's cheek, then jogged away, his white shepherd's costume flapping around his booted ankles.

Cherry felt slighted that he didn't kiss her, too.

What in the world was she thinking? She'd been silently lamenting being uncomfortable with public attention and fussing. Having this sexy cowboy living in her house was wearing on her nerves. And her sanity!

As soon as everyone was in place, cars began to make the loop from Main Street through the church parking lot, driving slowly to take in the live nativity scenes and listen to the Christmas hymns. If they wanted, they could end at the refreshment booth for a hot drink passed through the car window. Some would simply park and walk the route.

A huge crèche, built by local contractor, Jake McCall, was the focal point of the attraction. A bright star appeared to float above it. People from all over the county and as far away as Billings lined the street with cars and pickups, cruising by to view the Christmas scene.

The sets were built by most of the ranchers, each donating their time and materials. Portable heaters kept the animals warm and the cabin size wood structures kept the snow off them and the characters. Camels, some as tall as seven feet, stood looking bored to death. Others lay on the ground, knobby knees bent beneath them. Clay held the lead rope to the donkeys. A choir of angels sang Christmas hymns, flash-lights hidden beneath their silver wings to give a glow to their wings and halos.

In recent years, they'd used one of the new babies in town —or several of them on different shifts—as the live baby Jesus. Just because Cherry hadn't attended didn't mean she hadn't eavesdropped on every conversation she'd been within earshot of. Cherry could tell which baby was nestled in the soft, blanketed hay by the mother playing the part of Mary. Tonight, it was Eden Stratton, so the swaddled infant was more than likely her newest baby boy, William.

Seated comfortably beneath the concession tent, Cherry was being highly entertained by Mildred and Opal's good-natured bickering when Clay walked up. Not a donkey in sight. She'd been keeping such a close eye on him—surrepti-tiously, of course—she wasn't sure how she'd missed seeing him leave his post.

"Change of plans, Red. Eden's not feeling well and they need a stand-in for Mary and Joseph. It's perfect for you with your injury because you'll be sitting, so I volunteered us."

"Oh, Clay, you shouldn't—"

"Too late, Sugar. We need to hurry before Eden changes the holy night story and barfs on the crèche."

"Oh, dear," Mildred said. "I wonder if that sweet girl is with child again. Wouldn't that be wonderful?"

"Now, sister," Opal said. "Don't go starting rumors. That baby boy of theirs is barely out of the womb." But both sisters looked extremely pleased by the prospect of another possible baby on the way.

Cherry snagged her cane and moved up next to Clay. He put a steadying arm around her and guided her through the snowy path toward the manger set. She'd refused to try to navigate the event on crutches, which was purely a vanity issue on her part—and the unreasonable need to not look weak and clumsy in the eyes of her neighbors.

She really needed to quit this continued worry over being judged. Her leg was hurting like mad, and trying to disguise her limp and not rely on the cane was making matters worse, and becoming ridiculous.

"Thank you so much for coming," Eden said the moment they showed up. She whipped the simple white costume—which was little more than a sheet tied at the waist—over her head and slipped it over Cherry's. "All you need to do is sit right here and mind the baby."

"*Your* baby?" Cherry squeaked. Good Lord, she *never* squeaked!

"Yes, he's sound asleep. And Clay can scoop him up if he wakes. I just need to lie down for a few minutes and catch my breath."

Clay touched the other woman's arm. "Need me to go get Chance?"

Yes, Cherry thought, staring at the baby. Someone should go get the doctor.

"Heavens no," Eden said with a laugh. "I imagine I'm just sleep-deprived. I'll be fine. And I so appreciate y'all steppin' in for me."

Cherry's gaze snapped up at Eden's cheerful tone. She smelled a setup, especially when Eden grabbed her husband by the arm—who'd already transferred his Joseph costume to Clay—and hustled him out of the set.

"She's just going to leave her little baby with us like this?"

Clay grinned. "Can't get in too much trouble if he's sleeping."

"But what if he wakes up? Isn't that a little irresponsible of

Eden to *abandon* the little thing like this with perfect strangers?"

"Sugar." He said it softly, gently. "We're not strangers. And I've done my fair share of babysitting for my nieces and nephews. Eden and Stony know they've left their little one in good hands."

"*Your* hands, maybe," she said grudgingly and couldn't help peeking beneath the blanket at the sweet little cherub face sleeping so soundly.

Clay watched her, saw her yearning. The sadness and *longing* that came over her made him wonder if he'd made a mistake by agreeing to Eden's scheme. He'd thought this would be a great way for her to mingle with the community while staying off her feet. He hadn't expected her silent reaction, the raw, naked flash of bittersweet pain.

He gave her a moment to settle, felt himself relax when she no longer looked like she'd shatter. That was something he had *never* associated with Cherry Peyton. She wasn't a woman to show vulnerabilities. Those few seconds had been totally unnerving.

Still, the question burning inside of him wouldn't be silenced. "I've seen you with every baby animal and stray in the county. You're meant to nurture. How come you never had kids of your own?" he asked.

She tucked the blanket more securely around the baby. The space heaters in the cabin-sized manger kept the space plenty warm. She shook her head. "I gave up on that dream a long time ago."

Now he was even more confused. Her aloof personality might convey to outsiders that she wasn't into kids—just working her ranch and animals. Her nurturing side belied that. Now her words hinted at heartache. For the life of him, he couldn't stop himself from prying. He wanted to know this woman from the inside out.

And he wanted to know if their goals aligned. Because he'd never thought he wanted a family but recently, seeing his brothers' and friends' happiness, he'd started to yearn. He was at a time in his life where he had a satisfying career working Callahan and Sons ranch and the horses, and more money than he knew what to do with. But he wanted more. He wanted a family of his own.

"So, you don't have anything against children, but you don't plan to include them in your future?"

"Can't." She said it softly, sadly, her blue-eyed gaze raising from the sleeping baby to lock with his.

The renewed anguish that flashed in her eyes was so evident he swore he could feel her pain. The sensation lodged beneath his breastbone and spread like a swarm of stinging wasps. This woman was literally breaking his heart.

CHAPTER 5

*S*now fell again overnight. Clay figured at this rate, they were definitely assured of a white Christmas—maybe even *too* white. Snow drifts would make it difficult to get to Christmas Eve service at the church. That was still three weeks away, so no sense borrowing trouble.

Then again, the neighbors were rarely worried about breaking out the snowmobiles or pulling wagons hooked to sleds to get where they needed to be if the four-wheel-drives weren't up to the job. Natives took the weather in stride. It was only the newcomers in town who worried over it. Clay thought about Hannah Malone—hell, even his own sisters-in-law were having to adjust to life with Montana winters.

Cherry didn't seem to mind—even though she'd grown up in Texas which had a much milder climate. He'd seen her out in blizzard conditions riding fence and gathering stray cows who'd wandered too far, helping the neighbors round up theirs. She wasn't afraid of hard work and mostly kept to herself. Which was why her sadness had slayed him so thoroughly the other night at the nativity drive-through.

She was such a contrast—aloof, capable rancher and nurturer. When it came down to it, that's what this ranch was to her. Nurturing. He doubted she realized it. She loved that darned bull and every cow and calf on the property as though they were pets. Then there were the strays she took in.

He looked up when he heard Ethan's white Ford coming up the road, a snowplow hooked to the front bumper. The truck had four-wheel drive and extra high clearance, as well as the after-market snow scoop attached to the front end. Nobody would catch him stuck in a snowbank.

"Hey, bro," he called when Ethan stopped and opened the door. "You bringing me Christmas presents?"

Ethan stepped out with a small cardboard box. "Not for you. This is for Cherry."

"I might have to object to you bringing my lady gifts."

"Your lady, huh? That serious?"

Clay shrugged. "If I had my way it would be. The lady in question is resisting."

Ethan's brow raised. "I'm sure I don't need to have the *respectful* talk with you, right? I mean you're practically living here."

Clay laughed out loud. "Right. Coming from the number one town playboy."

"*Reformed* playboy, if you please. I have a husband and father reputation to protect."

Clay moved forward to peek in the box. He knew Ethan was kidding with him. Fred Callahan had instilled respect and manners in all three of his sons. They all had an ingrained code of how to treat a woman, and they were strict about it.

When he pulled back the old towels, two little black kittens peered up at him. "Whoa. Tiny little suckers. Where'd you get them?"

"Coyotes got the mama cat. I saw him trotting off with her from the hangar early this morning. Later on, I got a gut feeling and went looking to see if there were more varmints hanging around. Found these two instead. I couldn't take them in the house because Katie would have vibrated with excitement, and Dora's got enough on her plate right now with her folks coming in for Christmas. Since we usually bring Cherry all our strays, I thought she'd be the best bet. What do you think? Is she up to it?"

As he'd just been thinking, the whole town knew of Cherry's softer side—despite the walls she erected.

"She's hobbling around, but she's moving better. Refuses to use the crutches. Insists she's fine. She even used a horse poultice on her calf."

Ethan grinned. "She's a tough gal. And resourceful."

"Mmm."

Ethan gave him a shrewd look. "You doing okay? I know you have feelings for Cherry. We've all known it a while now. But she's been through a lot."

Clay lightly punched his brother on the shoulder. "Thanks for worrying over my heart."

"Well, it's a thing, you know?"

"Yeah, I know." It was a real thing that his heart could get broken. "She's worth the chance, though."

"Then, good luck to you. If she can't keep the kittens, let me know and I'll drop them off with Lyle. I almost took them there in the first place, but figured Cherry would have a better bedside manner."

"Better than the vet?" He didn't have to think about that too hard.

"He's not in the clinic twenty-four-seven. I figured these guys would need round the clock care for a little bit."

"Yeah, you're right. We might have to call him if the kittens fail to thrive, but I'm pretty sure Cherry will know what to do."

"She usually does. Call if you need anything." Ethan got in the truck and drove off.

Clay made his way into the kitchen where Cherry was standing by the stove.

"I have a delivery for you."

He walked over to her and she peeked inside the blanket. "Oh, sweet babies. They can't be more than three or four weeks old. Hang on."

She hop-stepped out of the room before he could stop her.

"What do you need," he asked, following on her heels, exasperated that he could barely keep up—and *she* was the one with the injured leg.

"I've got it."

Stubborn woman. She grabbed a heating pad out of the hall closet, some towels, and a hot water bottle, then took the shivering little kittens from him. "Poor sweethearts," she crooned. "Here, go put some hot water in this."

She handed him a rubber bladder that looked older than him. "Should I call Lyle Watkins?" Clay asked.

"Let me assess them before we waste his time. These babies look healthy enough—although they're cold. Their little bodies don't regulate on their own, so we'll warm them up a bit. You sure there's no mama kitty? They go off and leave their babies sometimes, but they usually return."

"Ethan saw a coyote carry her off."

"Oh, poor thing. I'm surprised Dora didn't scoop these littles up. She seems to adore anything tiny so she can take her pictures."

"Ethan said it was too much for them. Figured they'd need

round the clock feedings, and Dora doesn't have experience with that."

"Well, her brother is the vet. I'm surprised she didn't call him."

"To tell the truth, Ethan didn't give her the opportunity. He felt it was more than she needed to add to her plate, so he automatically brought them over here to you."

"I don't have enough on *my* plate?" There was more amusement in her tone than bother.

"You have more experience. Everyone around here knows to bring you their strays to foster."

"Mmmm. These babies are so cute. Might be difficult to rehome them when the time comes."

Hope was poking her nose in the towel. The dog was a nurturer, just like her human. She was clearly dying to wrap her warm body around these babies. Joy, on the other hand, thought the new additions were going to be exuberant playmates. She was already in the play position, head down, butt in the air, tail wagging like mad.

Clay scooped her up. "Not for you, little jingle bells," he crooned and kissed the puppy's head. "These kittens are cold and too tiny to play."

As though understanding, the puppy gave him a quick lick on the cheek and settled happily in his arms.

"They look like they're about a month old. I image they were still nursing. I've got some kitten formula in the cupboard to the left of the sink."

"Of course you do," Clay said with a chuckle and rose to get it. He found tiny bottles, nipples and syringes next to the can of kitten formula.

"Looks like you're prepared."

"Like you said. Not my first rodeo. I think I'm going to try something different. I can put them in the laundry basket, but...Hope, come here and lay down." She led the dog closer to the fireplace. The sweet Lab knew exactly what she was being asked. She laid on her side and Cherry snuggled the two kittens up against her. Hope stared down at the mewling creatures with what looked like canine motherly love.

"Darndest thing," Clay said.

"She's a great assistant when it comes to caring for abandoned animals. It's like she has a sense for the underdog. Or under *kitten* in this case."

She tucked the heating pad on the other side of the kittens so they were surrounded by both Hope's heat as well as the artificial heat. "I want to make sure their body temperature gets back to normal as soon as possible. No telling how long they've been out in the snow. It's a wonder they aren't frozen stiff." She clucked and worried as she arranged the small fluff balls to her liking, stroking Hope and praising the Lab.

"Ethan found them in one of the outbuildings behind the hangar. So at least they were somewhat out of the elements."

"And there were just the two?"

"Yes. He said he looked through the whole shed. This is it."

"I'll need to feed them every two or three hours until we're sure they're stabilized."

"We."

She looked up. "What?"

"*We* will feed them. In fact, we'll take shifts. You're still recuperating and need your rest."

His bossiness gave her a jolt. But only for a split second. He was just being Clay. When would she ever not have this knee-jerk reaction?

"Have you ever raised a newborn kitten?"

"Nope. Raised a foal and a puppy, though."

"Without their mama?"

"Well, no. The mamas were present."

"In this case, we get to be the mama. Isn't that right, sweetheart," she crooned, stroking the closest kitten.

For a minute, Clay thought she was talking to him. Wishful thinking, for sure. One day, he promised himself. One day she would call him sweetheart.

"You going to name them?"

She shrugged. "Probably."

"I thought most fosters didn't name them for fear of getting too attached."

"I get attached regardless. Might as well help shape their personalities with a name. They can't all be baby kitty."

"So, what are you thinking?"

"Hmm. Something Christmassy. Gender neutral, since I'm not sure if we've got girls or boys." She'd looked and couldn't tell because they were so young. "Maybe Jingle and Kris"

"Chris?"

"Kris Kringle," she clarified. "Here, come sit and make sure everyone stays put while I fix some bottles."

He still held Joy in his arms as he eased on the floor beside Hope. Carefully, he set the puppy down and monitored her to make sure she wouldn't pounce. After a little coaching, Joy was sniffing respectfully at the kittens, then settling at a safe distance to watch. Smart little thing. She was learning so fast. Anything he tried to teach her, she picked up immediately. This was one stray he imagined Cherry would have some trouble parting with. He'd already noticed that no matter her pain level, she was constantly cuddling the little dog. Heck, he might even adopt Joy himself since he was half in love with the little menace.

After mixing and warming the bottles, Cherry returned to

the fireplace and eased down beside him. He saw her wince, and knew she was doing too much—not just her leg, but her healing ribs as well. Before he could admonish, she thrust one of the bottles at him.

"Choose a kitten and let's get some nourishment into those little bodies."

"Okay, I got Jingle. And hopefully Joy won't get jealous because I sometimes call her Jingle Bells."

Cherry smiled and cradled the other kitten. Hope got up, sniffing both to make sure they were doing things right.

"You're good at this," he said, watching the delighted, loving expression on her face as she held the bottle to the small kitten's mouth. As the kitten sucked, it wiggled its little ears. It was the cutest darn thing.

"I love animals. I grew up around them, especially horses. During my teen years, I competed in barrel racing. Then I went off to college and studied animal sciences." She wiped the kitten's mouth, where the formula was dripping. "I always wanted to work with them in some capacity. I'd thought maybe veterinary."

"What happened?"

"I met Dell. He was a rodeo cowboy. Older than me. A party boy. Charming." She looked up at him. "You knew him."

Clay raised a brow but didn't comment. Yes, he'd known Dell—not well, of course, since the other man had been several years older than him—but in small towns like Shotgun Ridge, everyone knew of everyone else.

It was rare for Cherry to even talk about her past, and he didn't want to derail her. He simply listened, ignoring the formula that was creating a wet spot on his jeans where the kitten rested on his thigh, sucking at the nipple and letting half of the liquid run out of its mouth.

"My parents weren't crazy about him—especially since he was veering me from a career path. But I fell for him, and we ended up married before my folks could talk sense into me."

"Marriage didn't have to end your career aspirations," he said carefully.

"Dell was still traveling the rodeo circuit, and I wanted to be free to go with him. Then he got hurt and couldn't work for a while. All he could think about was coming here. I don't know why, really. He had no one here—his parents passed away before we were even married. But he was adamant that we were going to move to Shotgun Ridge. My parents were worried that we wouldn't be able to survive, but they were somewhat comforted that that I'd at least have some family close by—Uncle Ozzie had lived here since he and Aunt Vanessa married. So, as a late wedding gift—that's what they called it so Dell wouldn't get his masculine feelings all twisted up—they gave me Casanova and Uncle Ozzie just *happened* to call and offer us the house and land here. He said he'd planned to will it to me anyway, and no sense waiting until he was pushing up daisies to see me enjoy it. Daddy made sure the papers for the land and buildings and Casanova were deeded in my name only."

"Smart parents, since Montana isn't a community property state when it comes to divorce."

"Well, there was no divorce, but it made things much easier when Dell died."

"He pretty much ran things into the ground, didn't he," Clay said, more of a statement than a question. He'd been watching Cherry Peyton from afar for the past six years, and one thing he'd always known was that Wendell Payne hadn't deserved her.

He saw the flash of discomfort in her striking blue eyes,

gone nearly before it had even appeared. "I tried to keep up. But he was pretty contrary. If I said the sky was blue, he'd insist it was pink and accuse me of deliberately trying to piss him off. If I offered a suggestion regarding the upkeep of the buildings or livestock, he'd shut me down and tell me he had it handled, and accuse me of thinking he couldn't do stuff. I went around him as much as I could, but some things weren't worth the effort of an argument. It was the alcohol."

"Don't make excuses for him, Sugar."

"I'm not—well, maybe I am. But it was a fact of life. If I'm honest, I'll admit that I'm a little bitter that I ended up having to borrow against the ranch to keep us on track. I started out owning it free and clear but that's not the case anymore. But I've managed to pay the feed bill and keep the utilities on. And until not too long ago, I'd hung on to Casanova."

He shifted the kitten who'd fallen asleep on his thigh and placed it in the laundry basket among the soft cushion of towels. "It's not like you lost the bull. You still have him. At least fifty-one percent of him anyway. And Wyatt would never try to mess with you on the partnership. He's a solid guy and a solid businessman."

She sighed and settled her kitten in the laundry basket next to its sibling. "I know that Wyatt's a good man. It's my pride."

"Cherry, you've done a great job with this ranch. Both with the handicap of a drunk husband, and now as a single woman doing it all. I'm pretty much in awe of you."

She doubted he'd be in awe if he knew the whole truth. She pushed herself up from the floor, kept that thought to herself. "Thanks."

"Although I *do* find your stubbornness unnecessary." He also got to his feet, standing directly in front of her. The fire crackled and popped, warming the room. She was so close he could smell the cherry scent of her lotion. Her blue eyes held a slight hint of vulnerability. It would be so easy to lean down and take her mouth with his. It took everything within him to resist. At least until she invited him in.

"You know I want to kiss you, right?" His words were gravelly even to his own ears, and he swore he could hear his heartbeat.

"Not a good idea."

"You've said that before. Why?"

"Clay, for one thing, I'm older than you."

"Are you *joking*?" He hadn't been prepared for that argument, hadn't even thought about it. He knew she'd recently turned forty—that information had leaked when she'd dropped her driver's license at the general store and his sister-in-law Abbe had happened to retrieve it for her. "Now you're just grabbing at straws. You're going to hold five measly birthdays against me? Sugar, I'm not some twenty-year-old with no life experience. Hell, I probably had more life experience in the first five years of my life than most people have in forty years."

She surprised him by putting her palm on his chest, right over his heart. As if she knew the reminder of his past had caused a knee-jerk flash of pain. He took advantage and placed his hand over hers, holding her to him. His other hand cupped her cheek, slid beneath her hair.

"Oh, to hell with it." He lowered his head and kissed her.

He would have stopped in a heartbeat if she'd resisted. But she didn't. She eased right into him and participated, her lips opening beneath his, her body pressing closer. He held her gently, poured as much emotion as he could into that single kiss, telling her with his lips and his body and his actions that she was special. Cherished.

When he lifted his head, their eyes clung. He swept her bangs from her forehead where a faint bruise still marred her smooth skin, trailed his fingers over her peaches and cream cheek. She had the typical coloring of a redhead. Fair skin, vivid blue eyes, cheeks that couldn't hide a blush. Her body was fit and strong. She was a man's dream. She was definitely *his* dream. Had been for some time now.

Before he'd identified that he wanted a wife and family—complements of the matchmaker's meddling in Ethan and Grant's lives—he'd stuck to long distance, surface relationships. No one had ever really engaged his heart. He had a fulfilling life, a great career, plenty of money, and female companionship with no strings whenever he wanted. In the past couple of years, work and family and fantasies about the newly widowed Cherry had eliminated the enticement of those superficial relationships.

Then he'd kissed Cherry under a sprig of mistletoe and he'd been one and done.

In his arrogance, he'd assumed she would automatically fall in step with his future vision.

A huge miscalculation on his part.

She broke the connection of their gaze and stepped back. He let her go—for now. He'd pushed about as hard as he should for the time being.

"I'll go fix us some dinner. Settle in and we'll eat by the fire. It's going to be a long night with the little orphans."

"Clay, you've been doing so much. I can fix my own dinner."

"I imagine you can." He gave her hand a squeeze. "But

would it be okay with you if I do it? I kind of like creating in the kitchen."

"And you're impatient with my slowness?"

He bit his lips but couldn't hide a smile. "I didn't say that, Sugar. You did."

She smiled at him and relaxed on the sofa. "Be my guest. Cook away."

~

AFTER SUPPER, Clay went out to check on the animals and settle them in for the night. Cherry fed the kittens again and snuggled them in the laundry basket by the fire. Hope, her head on her paws, lay next to the basket, warming herself and keeping watch over the kittens and the sleeping puppy. Joy was tuckered out and lay on her back with her legs relaxed in the air, full of trust and adorableness—and not a speck of female modesty.

It gave Cherry a tender sense of purpose and happiness to care for these sweet animals. They needed her. Depended on her. And she liked that feeling.

She eased down on the couch and pulled the crochet afghan over her legs. It had been several hours since Clay had spontaneously kissed her, and she wasn't sure her heart had actually settled yet. What was she thinking? She wasn't really. She was operating on emotions. On *feelings*.

Clay made her feel safe and cared for—or as safe as she could feel around someone else. A man at least. But she had so much work to do on herself, so many demons to slay and questions to answer about the type of woman she'd become, and the type of woman she wanted to be.

Sometimes, she wished she could go back to being the

princess of the barrel racing community, the confident girl who made the plans for all her friends and never thought about her actions or second-guessed her decisions or who she was. She'd been a leader, not a follower.

Living with Dell had made her question that girl. Because, if she really thought about it, she'd been a bit controlling and bossy. It had felt like a strong quality at the time. Now she wondered if she'd hurt anyone. She hid behind aloofness, but inside her head, she was still a bit of a mess. And she couldn't seem to get past it. Wasn't sure how to take that final step to heal. Because healing meant revealing everything she'd endured. And the thought made her choke every time.

She felt the cold air whoosh in when Clay opened the door. Hope looked up with a scolding expression in her big brown eyes, then settled again.

He removed his hat and coat, then came to sit beside her on the couch, slipping part of the blanket over his knees as though they shared the furniture like this all the time. It was such a natural move, it made her want to wallow in it for a moment. He really was a special man. Strong. Kind. Sexy. Lord, was he sexy.

And she should not be thinking about that. She had enough trouble not dwelling on that kiss they'd shared before dinner. Because she wanted—badly—to kiss him again, she decided they needed a distraction.

She wasn't normally one to pry into someone else's business, but she really wanted to know Clay. On the deepest level.

"Earlier, you said something about life experience before you were five..." She let her voice trail off, hoping he'd pick up the conversation. He did.

"Mmm. I hadn't expected that memory to jump up and bother me. I had a good life with Dad."

"You mean Fred?"

"Yes. He's the only father I ever knew. And the best, that's for sure. I miss him like mad, and I rarely think about the time before he adopted us."

"I've heard plenty about him over the years."

"I'm not surprised. Everyone around here loved and respected him. Cancer got him. About a year before you moved here."

"I wish I could have met him."

"He'd have liked you."

"He never married?"

"Didn't seem inclined. He spent every ounce of his being on us boys and our business."

"Which is pretty vast, if rumor serves you."

"Listening to rumors, hmm?" He shifted on the couch, draped his arm over her shoulders and pulled her against him. For a bare instant, she resisted.

"Might as well get comfy," he said as though it was no big deal. Actually, any time he had her in his arms was a big deal.

"I don't think what folks say about you and your brothers are rumors." She tucked her legs up on the couch, leaned into him, and picked up the conversation as though there'd never been a pause. "I know you breed prized stock and champion racehorses."

"Yes. We're involved in a little more than just breeding—although the value of that end of the operation is nothing to sneeze at. We have an unrivaled reputation for consistently turning out champions that win big bucks in racing, so buyers pay top dollar for stud services *and* our foals. We've also got our own horses we run at various racetracks—that's mostly my area of expertise. The rest of our financial dealings are in cattle—which we're phasing out—and the stock market."

"How in the world do you keep up with it all?"

"Ethan and Grant and I have pretty much worked out a system. We each have our strengths. We work well together, but we also automatically do our own chores, and it keeps everything clicking. Plus, we've got quite a few employees to pick up the slack."

"Which is why you're able to just take off and spend all this time over here? I feel bad that you're doing my work and ignoring your own."

"Have you heard anyone complaining?"

"Well, I doubt they'd complain to me. So, how old were you when you came to Shotgun Ridge?"

"Not quite five." He cast his mind to a time that he rarely thought about anymore. It was part of who he was, though, and he wanted Cherry to know. "I was born in Chicago and spent the first few years of my life there. My mom was married three times, and my brothers and I all have different fathers—more accurately, sperm donors. Ethan and I don't have any idea who ours are, but Grant recently found out about his biological dad. You heard about that, right?"

"A little. I was part of the search party when the Vegas crime mob came after Abbe and Jolene. That was pretty scary. I didn't pry into the details, though."

"Abbe's adoptive father, Stewart Shea, was a mob boss who was trying to get out of the business. When the mob put a hit on Abbe's fiancé—Jolene's father—and killed him in front of Abbe, they threatened Jolene if Abbe talked. She'd found papers stating that Stewart was Grant's biological father. Stewart had followed Grant's life and had a whole dossier on him. Abbe read it and figured he was the best person to keep her and her daughter safe. And she'd decided that since he was the closest thing she could call family, she was going to leave Jolene with him and disappear."

"That's quite a sacrifice."

"Yeah, but Grant wasn't going for it. And neither were we. We knew between the three of us, plus this town, that we could keep Abbe and Jolie safe. We nearly miscalculated, but it all worked out."

"And does Grant have a relationship with his father—the biological one—now?"

"Stewart, along with Abbe's mother, Cynthia, are in the Witness Protection Program. Grant and Abbe visited after Faith was born, but it's not as though they can have a physically close relationship."

"I'm glad there's no animosity. And I'm sure it doesn't take away from Fred at all."

"No. Nothing could ever sully that bond. Fred Callahan was our father in every sense of the word except for biology. Anyway, in addition to the husbands, our mother lived with several men. Some of them not so nice. We were on a road trip with one of her boyfriends—who made it clear that he hadn't signed on for three little kids—when our mom dropped us off at social services in Idaho and forgot to come back for us."

Cherry gasped. "Forgot?"

"That's just me being polite. Ethan was eight, and Grant was six and I wasn't quite five. The lady at social services was nice. I still remember her name. Mrs. Lovell. It clearly broke her heart to tell us our mom wasn't coming for us. She tried to ease into it, claiming it would be just for a little while, but that she needed to find a place for us to stay. Ethan had all kinds of attitude, saying there was no way he'd let us be separated. Mrs. Lovell made a few phone calls and we found ourselves out on Bernie Treechman's farm."

"Well, at least you were together."

"Mmm. He seemed like a good enough man—had a wife and a son who was about Grant's age. As soon as Mrs. Lovell left, it was clear that he only wanted foster kids to use as free labor on his ranch."

"But you were four!"

"Old enough to hold a shovel or a hoe. We stuck together, me and my brothers, and we tried to shield Scott—Treechman's son—from as much of the nastiness as we could. Scott was kind of frail and his father hated that about him. One day, Fred Callahan came out to buy some horses, and he saw us, and ended up buying us."

"He *bought* you?"

"Yes. He gave Treechman money. Then he enlisted the help of your Uncle Ozzie and the rest of the town so he wouldn't get hit with kidnapping charges for taking us across state lines without approval, and petitioned the courts to legally adopt us. He was a bachelor—and remained one until he died —and didn't know much about raising kids. But he knew about love. And he gave that to us in spades."

"You were lucky."

"Yes. He had his work cut out for him. I was little, but Ethan—being the oldest—felt it was his responsibility to take care of us. He was angry and quite a handful and didn't trust anyone—and Grant and I pretty much took our cues from him, so we weren't any picnic either. But Fred Callahan had the patience of a saint."

She sighed and eased closer to him, not even realizing she was doing so.

"Although I was little," he said, "I'll never forget arriving in

81

Shotgun Ridge and my first impression of the Callahan Farm, all the white fences and miles of green grass and white buildings and horses. It was peaceful. Odd that I could sense that even at first glance. Maybe not so odd, because before Treechman, we were used to living in rundown apartments and hanging out in alleyways in the worst parts of Chicago. Ethan did odd jobs for the landlord and made Grant and I collect bottles and cans for recycling. Our mom disappeared for days at a time. Ethan got pretty good at picking pockets. He wouldn't let me or Grant steal, and he only did it to feed us. He made sure we knew it was wrong and that only he could do it under special circumstances because he was the oldest."

"I can't even imagine," she said. "I had amazing parents and never felt unsafe a day in my life growing up." That feeling had only come after she'd been married.

"You were lucky. But it turns out, so were me and my brothers. It was as if Fred Callahan was sent straight from Heaven to save us. So, when I first laid eyes on this town and the Callahan farm, all the openness and beauty and nature gave me a sense of belonging. Maybe because I was younger, but I took to Fred and the town and this way of life right away and it would have taken a whole lot for Ethan to talk me into leaving."

"That's sweet. How long did it take Ethan to come around?"

He smiled. "A while. Then one day, Fred sat us down and asked our permission to adopt us. He'd had to track down our mom who was more than happy to sign away her rights. The day the courts finalized the papers and our names were changed to Callahan, some of the neighbors had hung the sign Dad had special ordered so it was up when we drove home. It said, 'Callahan and Sons'. I remember that Ethan cried. That was the turning point. And from then on, we had a good life. Still do."

"And your mom? Did you ever see her again?"

"No. She died when I was fourteen. She'd married again—to a wealthy man this time—and was a rich widow. She willed all her money to us."

"Well, at least that's something."

"Ethan nearly had a fit, and the rest of us pretty much agreed. We didn't want anything to do with her or her money. But Dad convinced us to take the money. To use some of it to help other boys who had similar situations to ours. He helped us invest and grow the money, and we've continued to give away most of it to charities catering to children and animals."

Cherry laid her head on Clay's shoulder and snuggled next to him, pulling the blanket around them. His story disarmed her. She wanted to comfort him. She knew she shouldn't encourage this closeness, but she was too tired to fight either of their emotions. The kittens were safe in the laundry basket by the fire, fast asleep. As were both the dogs.

Listening to Clay's recounting of his childhood and what had shaped him gave her even more respect for him. It explained a lot about his personality, his willingness—or need—to fight for the underdog, to take care of others. To take care of her.

She felt his fingers in her hair, idly stroking. He never missed an opportunity to touch her and she was starting to like it too much, to count on it, even. She turned her head, looked into his eyes.

His lips were so close. He was so easy to be with. Everything about him felt right. But could she trust her own judgment?

His head began to lower. She ought to move, yet was trapped in his gaze, in her own want. And she *did* want him.

An odd sound penetrated the edges of her mind, snapping her from the brink of reckless abandon. There was definitely a commotion going on outside. It took her a moment to realize what it was.

CHAPTER 6

*S*inging? What in the world?

And then it dawned on her. It was a Shotgun Ridge tradition for all the neighbors to gather and go to each other's houses caroling, then end up at the church for a cookie exchange.

They'd come to Cherry's house one year to carol and try to get her and Dell to join in, but Dell had been drunk so Cherry, who'd seen them coming, had turned off all the lights and pretended not to be home. Surely, the neighbors would have known they were home. Where else would they be? They hadn't come the next year. Cherry wondered if her Uncle Ozzie had advised the neighbors to leave them be.

It had always been easier on her when there wasn't change in their lives. Change of any kind gave Dell an excuse to get drunker—and Cherry was the one who had to put up with the behavior his secret binges created.

This year, though, when she heard the voices outside the door singing *Silent Night*, she didn't rush to turn off the lights. She looked at Clay and he grinned.

"Neighbors are here," he said as though they hadn't been about to indulge in mad passion. "Best get our coats."

"I'm not going anywhere." Her brain was clearly a little sluggish, but weren't they just supposed to stand at the door and listen?

"Sure, you are. I'll carry you if need be, but the hay wagon or snowmobile will be fun." He got up and opened the door, snagging his heavy leather coat on the way.

Cherry followed, feeling a bit of uncertainty mixed with a giddiness she hadn't felt in ages. It looked as though the entire town was on her porch and front lawn.

Eden Stratton played her guitar, the fingers cut out of her wool gloves so she could pick out the strings. Grant tossed a harmonica to Clay. He snagged it in mid-air and, without missing a beat, joined Eden in instrumentals.

Cherry felt even more emotions well inside her. This is what Christmas was all about. Families. Neighbors. Community. Love. She'd been totally out of her comfort zone attending the live nativity the other night. But if she was honest with herself, she'd loved every minute of it, felt something inside of her thawing at last.

Snow fell gently, adding to the already thin layer sticking to the ground. The colored lights decorating every space of eaves on her house and barn reflected off the white snow like drops of candy.

She shoved her feet into her boots by the door, then donned her coat, not even surprised when Clay paused with his harmonica to steady her. The fire had died to embers and the animals were all perfectly safe to leave—Clay had pretty much puppy-proofed the house.

She looked at him—his sexy smile and his obvious joy at the spontaneity of the season. Then her gaze touched on each one of her neighbors. She *wanted* so badly. What? She wasn't sure she could define it. Love, yes. To be able to trust so easily. To laugh so easily. To join in.

She'd held herself on the outside for so long, she didn't know how to break the pattern.

Clay, on the other hand, was determined to *teach* her how to break those patterns. He slid the harmonica in his pocket and swept her into his arms, carrying her off the porch and into the moonlight among the neighbors.

My gosh, everyone was watching! Her immediate reaction was to object. He didn't give her a chance.

Hannah clucked at him to be careful of Cherry's leg.

Dora clapped and said, "Yes, sir! Get that girl out here to help us sing. These men are getting a little off key!"

Cherry didn't know why she couldn't just observe from the porch, but the festive crowd won her over and she began to relax. Before she realized, Clay's baritone was close to her ear. "Come on, Red. You know the words."

The challenge was there. And so hard to resist. She joined in a lively rendition of "Jingle Bells" and found herself having the time of her life.

Her Uncle Ozzie gave her a wink and stood off to the side with his buddies. The matchmakers. Cherry gave him a reluctant smile, hoping he wasn't getting any ideas where she was concerned—especially since it had been Clay who had opened her front door. Clearly the whole town knew he was staying with her, but still.

"I brought an extra snowmobile," Grant said to Clay. "Figured since Cherry's still a little gimpy, you can ride double."

"Ride where?" Cherry asked, her defenses automatically raising again.

"The church, of course," Clay said. "Cookie exchange. It's tradition."

"But I don't have cookies."

"Now you do," Eden Stratton said, stepping forward with a large Christmas tin. "I baked way too much and am gifting the extras to the neighbors."

"But then you'll be exchanging your own cookies," Cherry objected.

"No worries," Emily Bodine said. "She does this every year. And don't even think twice about accepting her offer. The twins keep me so busy and I'm not the greatest in the kitchen, so Eden came with several dozen in hand for me, too." She laughed and snuggled beneath Cheyenne's shoulder, who beamed at her with a love so bright it nearly lit up the yard.

Cherry reached for the Christmassy tin, incredibly touched that these neighbors—who she barely knew other than on the surface or through helping out with their cattle when it was time for round up or riding fence—were drawing her in this way.

The air was downright chilly, but invigorating. Maybe that was the excitement of being included. Clay settled her on the snowmobile, then produced a knitted wool scarf he'd obviously snagged from the hall-tree beside the front door, wrapping it around her neck and over the lower half of her face.

"You got gloves and a hat in the pockets of that coat?"

"Of course." She donned a wool stocking cap and leather gloves. They were work gloves, so she definitely wasn't making a fashion statement, but no one was standing around judging. She didn't know where that thought had come from. She'd never before felt vain about her outerwear.

"Hold tight," Clay said as he put the snowmobile in

motion. Headlights cut through the darkness of the night as they headed out across the field, bypassing the road, yet keeping pace with the trucks that *did* stick to the highway. They took it slow in deference to the horses pulling wagons. The whole point was to travel together in a sort of caravan, gathering neighbors as they went. Voices echoed in song and laughter, ringing through the crisp, clear night.

They stopped at Chance and Kelly Hammond's ranch and Cherry thought they would wait while the doctors and their little girls, Kimmy and Jessica, bundled up, but Kelly waved the singing crowd inside, where she passed out hot cider, then sat at the piano and began to accompany Eden's guitar and Clay's harmonica in several more carols. Cherry didn't have any trouble keeping up with the tunes. It was like revisiting her childhood all over again, and she was more than a little enchanted.

Leaving with the Hammonds, they ended up in town to gather up Mildred and Opal. Every house they'd stopped at was decorated to the rooftops, festive and bright. The Bagley sisters' tree was strung with white lights, lace, angels, and old-fashioned tinsel, and sat on an antique table in the corner of their front parlor so it could be viewed by all who passed by on Main Street. Gifts spilled off the surface of the table to the floor beneath, where a fat cat slept among the colorful bows and ribbons, not even flinching at the rowdy crowd. After eating way too many cookies and hot cocoa, they deposited the sisters in Stony's Suburban to continue the journey.

The last stop on their singing tour was the home of Dan and Amy Lucas—the pastor and his wife. They lived behind the church where the cookie exchange was to take place.

"We're stopping at their house?" Cherry asked in Clay's ear

as they bypassed the church parking lot and pulled right up on the rectory's front lawn.

Clay eased the snowmobile to a stop and dismounted, helping Cherry do the same. "Sure. They don't want to miss out on folks coming to their door. You doing okay? Is this too much for you?"

"I'm fine." She realized that his worry didn't annoy her. It made her feel cherished. And she really shouldn't be fostering those thoughts or feelings. "Who starts the caroling if no one wants to miss out?"

"Your uncle, naturally." The older folks were all pulling up in their various trucks, claiming open vehicles in the dead of winter were for young people only.

Cherry leaned on Clay, letting him balance out her weight as she favored her leg.

That surprising sense of belonging swept over her again.

She had an idea this would be a Christmas she'd always remember.

IT WAS LATE when they got back to Cherry's house. They fed the kittens again, then tucked them in for the night and stoked the fire to ward off the chill. Cherry spent several minutes loving on Hope and Joy. The two animals were becoming so bonded, she hadn't even felt guilty about leaving them this evening. She could tell that they were both sleepy. With one last scratch to Hope's ears, she invited the Lab to curl up on her fluffy pillow by the hearth, then scooped up Joy and settled her in the nurturing curve of Hope's belly.

"You ought to get off your leg. I'm sure you're tired."

"Clay, don't fuss. My leg's fine."

He stepped up so close she automatically took a half step back.

"Why do you do that?"

She knew what he was talking about, and she just couldn't explain it to him. A doctor in one of the emergency rooms she'd ended up in after a particularly ugly fight with Dell had talked to her a little bit about PTSD. She'd thought that was silly, figuring PTSD was reserved for veterans who'd been through unspeakable things serving their country, then she'd done some research. What she'd gone through with Dell had created trauma and stress. Thus, her knee-jerk reaction when anyone made a sudden move or took her out of her comfort zone.

She hated putting labels on herself.

And she didn't want to be that woman anymore.

Tonight had made her feel like a different person. A part of the community. A part of Clay's world.

And she'd liked the feeling.

Didn't want it to end.

Plus, being next to Clay Callahan all day and all evening was wearing on her nerves. He made her want in a way she hadn't wanted in years. She still didn't think she was the right woman for him. She had so much to work through before she could consider herself whole, but she was tired of fighting this attraction. What would it hurt to give in? What would it hurt to allow herself a night in his arms, to allow him to banish the ghosts of the past and create some new memories?

She would give anything to regain some of the feminine confidence she'd once had. And Clay Callahan was a sexy man. She had little doubt that he could help her heal—at least in the area of sex.

Deliberately, she retraced that half step, her breasts nearly brushing his shirt front. She ran her hands up his chest, rested them there, looked into his eyes.

"I'm not so great at relationships. I tend to retreat. It's kind of automatic."

"You don't need to retreat from me." His gaze dipped to her mouth, then back, his eyes locked on hers.

"I think I'm realizing that." She moved her hands higher, over his neck, brushing the hair at his nape.

He placed his hands at her hips, urged her the slightest bit closer. "And just so I'm not reading you wrong, you're not retreating now, right?" There was a question in his voice and in his eyes. And there was hope.

She wanted to give him that hope. And she loved that he was *asking*. Not *expecting*.

"No. I'm not retreating."

That was all the prompting he needed. He lowered his head and kissed her. His lips were warm and perfect. He was a good kisser, taking his time, nibbling and coaxing, never rushing. He urged her to participate. And she did.

She'd never had a kiss create such a reaction, such a desire. Just a simple meeting of lips and her body reacted like a stampede of horses was about to break through the front door. Her heart beat like mad and every nerve ending in her body tingled.

"You sure about this?" he asked, pressing his lips to her forehead, tilting her chin up so he could look into her eyes.

"Yes. I'm sure about this for right now."

He hesitated, as though to question her, then changed his mind and scooped her into his arms, carrying her into the bedroom.

He shut the bedroom door behind them, then eased her

feet to the floor, only breaking the kiss long enough to gently pull her thermal sweater over her head. His lips cruised over her chest, the gentle swell of her breasts above the scoop neck of her incredibly sexy black camisole. She didn't wear a bra—partly because of her healing ribs, and partly because she preferred the comfort and style. When she was bare from the waist up, he leaned back to just look.

"You are so beautiful. I knew you would be."

Cherry suffered a moment of unease. It had been a long time since a man had looked at her with such hunger and... and reverence. She wasn't sure a man had *ever* looked at her this way. It gave her a thrilling sense of power.

"You're a little overdressed." She unbuttoned his shirtfront, then pushed it off his shoulders and, bunching his t-shirt in her hands, pulled it up and over his head. She couldn't stop herself from smoothing her palms over his rock-hard chest. This man was incredibly made, so handsome and sexy. She pressed her lips to his chest, felt his hand in her hair, urging her mouth back up to his.

He kissed her deeply, warmly, until her head was spinning and her legs felt weak, then eased her onto the bed and pulled her jeans gently over her hips and legs.

His fingers grazed the bandage that still wrapped around her calf.

"I don't want to hurt you," he said, trailing sweet kisses over her stomach, her thighs, over the injury on her leg. *A kiss to make it better.*

She didn't know about healing, but his lips were definitely making her hot. Anticipation sizzled through her. For so many years, she'd lived a life of caution. Caution over what she said, what she did, right down to the expression on her face or her willingness to agree or disagree. She was so tired of keeping that caution strong. She wanted to forget—just for a while. She wanted to be the sexy, bold woman she'd once been, the woman who celebrated her sexuality and reveled in it.

His hold on her was firm, but Cherry didn't feel threatened. This was Clay, the man who cooked for her, arranged care and boarding for her horses, fixed her faucets, and bought her new appliances, all while catering to her every whim. He had a way of talking her into things that were right at the edges of her comfort zone.

And though making love with him was definitely pushing her comfort zone, a cattle stampede couldn't convince her to stop. She wanted him with a fervor that was almost frightening.

He lingered and nibbled and treated her as though she were made of the most delicate china. He kissed her until her soul sang, until her heart opened, and her senses nearly overloaded. For the strangest reason, she felt tears form behind her closed eyelids.

Ever in tune with her, he eased away, softly brushing her hair from her face, his body warm and heavy against hers, yet keeping any pressure away from her healing injuries.

"What is it?" he asked softly, his thumb catching the tear that squeezed from the corner of her eye.

She shook her head and gave a small laugh. "Stupid girl emotions. I'm actually horrified."

"Nothing wrong with girl emotions."

"I kind of pride myself on being a little stronger than that."

"Sugar, you're one of the strongest women I know. Do you want me to stop? I can. Just tell me that I can at least hold you through the night."

"I don't want you to stop, Clay. If you do, I might really fall apart."

He smiled, brushed his lips over the outside of her eye. "Can't have that. Tell me what you like."

"Mmm, you're doing a fine job." She trailed her lips over his neck, inhaled the clean masculine scent of man. "I…" She wasn't sure if she should continue.

"You can tell me anything, Sugar."

"I've never been kissed like that."

He went very still. She half expected him to pry. Instead, his gaze softened in a look so gentle, her heart leaped.

"Well, that's a crying shame. And it's my pleasure to make up for that lack. But, we'll take it slow."

"Not too slow." Cool sheets caressed her back as he shifted her, using his lips and hands to stroke her body to a fever pitch. She hooked her leg around his thigh and arched her hips against him. A scream of frustration built inside her. "I won't break, Clay."

That was all the urging he needed. The only way to describe his attention to her body was…he worshiped her. The first climax slammed into her with just the touch of his fingertips. The second came with his fingers deep inside of her and his lips cruising over her neck.

"Now, Clay," she said, hardly able to catch her breath.

He reached for his jeans on the floor, and she grabbed his arm, feeling the straining muscles of his biceps. She knew he was after a condom but didn't want to get into the reasons why that wasn't necessary. "We don't need that."

He paused for an instant. "I haven't been with another woman in two years," he said by way of assurance.

She hadn't been thinking about other relationships with regard to protection—only pregnancy. If she'd had her wits about her, she would have wondered why he hadn't been with anyone in so long. But at that moment, he kissed her and brought her back to the exquisite peak of desire before joining his body with hers.

Colors exploded behind her closed eyelids. Her body pulsed around him, throbbing, the desire so intense she thought she'd faint. And then he began to move, slowly at first, and then with increasing speed and friction. She braced her feet against the mattress, tilted her hips, and gave herself to him, every ounce of energy and emotion and pleasure that she could muster. Her world narrowed to the two of them. Just her. Just Clay. The slick friction of his skin against hers.

Pleasure built, soared. She could hardly catch her breath—and it wasn't from bruised ribs. With a final thrust, he sent her right over the edge of bliss, a bliss she'd never even known existed.

CHERRY WASN'T sure her heart would ever return to normal.

"You okay?"

"Mmm. Better than okay."

"I didn't mean to get so carried away."

"I think there's something to what they say about adrenaline taking away pain."

"Damn it, I knew you were in pain. I ought to be shot. Is it your ribs?"

She soothed him with a palm against his stubbly cheek, placing a soft kiss on his chin. "What ribs?"

He focused all his attention on her, his gaze landing everywhere as though examining an X-ray that would tell him if she were being honest.

"Really, Clay. I'm much better than fine. At the risk of inflating your ego, I'd have to say I'm amazingly fine."

He grinned and settled beside her, pulling the quilt over them, holding her naked body against the warmth of his. The contact made her ache anew—in an aroused way rather than pain.

"I'm all for you inflating my ego."

She kissed his chest, rested her head against his shoulder.

"So," he said, almost tentatively. "What was that about you not being kissed properly?"

"I guess I hadn't *realized* I'd never been kissed properly—until tonight."

"As much as I want to run with that statement and let my ego really take off, why the hell not?"

Cherry had always had a healthy attitude and appreciation for sex when she was young. It's what had attracted her to Dell, and what had kept them together in the beginning. Even when he'd started drinking and they'd started fighting, sex had been a way to make up—and she'd thought it was pretty good. Then Dell's drinking had gotten progressively worse, and so had his temper. Sex soon became a way to distract him, to keep the peace. Then it had become a chore, much like mucking out the stalls. She had to do it—at least if she wanted a few days of peace. Then it had become sickening, an act that she'd hated—nearly as much as she'd come to hate the man she was having it with.

Thinking the thought gave her a jolt, even though no one —Clay especially—could see inside her head.

Well, what they'd just done in this bed blew away anything she'd ever thought she knew or loved about sex. Clay was an unselfish lover. She'd never been on the receiving end of such tenderness, such mind-blowing pleasure.

"To be honest, my past experience has always been focused on the main event. Kissing was just a cue, you know? A way to signal we were on the path to sex. Once the cue was given, it was abandoned."

"That's awful. A kiss *is* the main event."

"Yes. You just showed me that. And I thank you from the bottom of my heart."

Clay felt like the luckiest man. He didn't want to spoil the mood, but questions were swirling in his head. Cherry was important to him, hell, he'd been half in love with her for years. If she hadn't been so stubborn and standoffish, he'd have pushed to have her in his bed much sooner. He idly stroked her shoulder, rubbed the ends of her silky red hair between his fingertips, inhaled the cherry fragrance lingering over her skin.

"You stopped me when I was reaching for protection. And the other night you mentioned not being able to have children. Can you talk about that?"

Her fingers stilled against his chest, then resumed their absent pattern, almost as though she were petting him. "I was married for almost fifteen years. We didn't use any form of birth control, and I never got pregnant."

"Did you consult a doctor?"

She sat up, pulling out of his arms, holding the sheet to her. He instantly regretted questioning her because he didn't want to lose the closeness they shared.

Instead of getting up, she grabbed a long t-shirt that was folded at the foot of the bed, pulled it over her head.

"I didn't mean to make you uncomfortable."

"You didn't. It's just...I'm not used to chatting it up in the buff."

He understood about feeling vulnerable. And making love, being naked with each other, was about as vulnerable as a couple could get. He respected her emotions enough to pull on his own clothes—at least his jeans, then sat on the bed, propped pillows behind them and pulled her next to him, ignoring her slight reluctance.

Ending up in bed together this soon hadn't been on his agenda. But since it had happened, he didn't want it to end. He should have kept the conversation light.

To his relief, she relaxed against him, idly stroking his chest as she admitted, "I didn't have any formal fertility tests, if that's what you're asking. But...well, I had an accident a while back—some trauma to my abdomen—and the internist made a few speculations."

"And you didn't pursue it?"

"I didn't see the need." She studied him for a full three seconds, her blue-eyed gaze cautious. "Why is it important whether or not I can get pregnant?"

He wanted to tread carefully here. "Well, I'm kind of thinking we're sort of a thing," he said, indicating the bed they were laying on. "So, that makes me want to know everything about you."

"Clay..." she raised up, twisted around to look at him more fully. "I didn't mean for this to happen. I'm not—"

He placed a finger against her lips. "Shh. I'm not asking you to give me a lifelong commitment—although if you want to offer, I'd surely accept." He grinned at her to lighten the mood. "But I do want to see where things can go with us. Can you give me that much?"

She took a deep breath. "I don't know. I told myself I'd never get involved with another man after Dell."

"Well, the horse is already out of the barn, don't you think?" He tried for his most charming smile.

She raised one perfectly arched red brow. "Pretty much."

"So, what do you say?"

Rather than answer with words, she leaned in and initiated a kiss that spoke to his very soul—and gave him hope.

CHAPTER 7

*C*herry overslept. Again. When she woke, she was alone in the bed.

She and Clay had made love again last night, but surely that didn't account for her inability to wake up before the sun as she usually did. Ranch life required a lot of long hours. And since she'd stopped the pain pills after the first day, there was no excuse for this laziness.

Now Clay was the one taking care of early morning chores. She noticed that the bedroom door was shut. Since the dogs weren't scratching to get in, she figured that was Clay's doing, making sure the animals wouldn't wake her.

She stretched, feeling cared for and happy. The minute the thought surfaced, she stilled. She couldn't get too used to this treatment. She was well on her way to healing. Soon, there would be no need for Clay to stay. It was important to her that she remained in control of her life. Allowing herself to wallow in the cozy emotions and fantasies of a special man taking care of her wasn't the path she needed to travel.

There were no guarantees in life. And the only person she

could truly count on was herself. She'd been doing a good enough job of that since Dell's death, and she didn't intend to alter her course. No matter how amazing last night had been.

Getting out of bed, she went to the bathroom, took a shower and changed the bandage on her leg. The nine-day-old wound was starting to heal and she wasn't as worried about it getting wet. As long as she dried it thoroughly, as she did now with the hair dryer, and re-wrapped it with the clean gauze, it shouldn't impede the healing process. She still felt a stinging jolt every time she took a step, but it was manageable and she didn't need the crutches, as long as she favored the leg and didn't put her entire weight on it.

Her ribs still smarted as well but since she had no intention of lounging indoors today, she hooked the stiff corset-style garment Chance had given her around her torso. It wasn't the most comfortable thing, but it lent a little support and gave her a better sense of security when she knew she'd be moving around and taking a stab at lifting hay and a saddle.

Because she was pretty determined to take Queenie for a ride and check on her herd. Poor Casanova must be thinking she'd abandoned him.

She dried her hair, and just holding the blow dryer above her head nearly sent her back to bed. She actually had to sit and rest for a minute.

Pulling on soft jeans, thick socks, her well-broken in boots, then both a thermal and flannel shirt, she made her way toward the kitchen. A banked fire sizzled behind the grate. The lights on the Christmas tree were on. Clay's doing? Or had they forgotten to turn them off last night? The smell of pine and the twinkle of lights and shiny ornaments gave her a soft, expectant feeling, like when she'd been a little girl running downstairs to see what Santa had left under the tree.

Hope jumped up from where she'd been laying in front of the kitten enclosure, her nails scratching on the scarred wooden floor.

"Hey, girl," Cherry said, giving the dog a hug. Not to be left out, Joy bounced around on her hind legs until Cherry picked her up to nuzzle her little ears. Chew bones and puppy toys were strewn across the floor. In the past, she'd kept the clutter of dog toys in the hall closet, but she no longer had to worry about anyone chastising her for leaving tripping hazards or messes.

She didn't know why she suddenly thought about Dell. Was it because of last night? She certainly didn't feel like she owed him any loyalty. She didn't feel any guilt over making love with Clay. At least not as far as Dell was concerned.

She *did* feel a tinge of unease that she could hurt Clay. She still didn't feel she was the right woman for him. And he clearly wanted more than just a friend—or a "friend with benefits"—relationship. He'd asked her if they could see where things went. And although she hadn't answered him with words, she'd as much as indicated she was willing by her actions.

Lord, was that so wrong?

Maybe. Because what if she couldn't get past her trust issues? It wasn't fair to Clay to constantly compare him to her past. She didn't consciously do that, but her unguarded moments were instinctive. Would he get tired of dealing with her inner ghosts? Her deep need to run the show? Her reactiveness?

And what about his questions about children? He could

easily find a woman in her prime childbearing years who could give him children.

She dismissed those thoughts, not wanting to dwell any more on her perceived inadequacies or shortcomings.

The kittens had graduated to a penned off area where they still had plenty of blankets for comfort, but also had access to a litter box. They were curled up on top of each other, sound asleep. A note was propped on top of the makeshift partition. "Fed Kris and Jingle already."

She smiled and set Joy on the floor, patting her leg so both dogs would follow her into the kitchen. She checked their food dishes and saw that Clay had already filled the water bowl, and there was another note on the counter that he'd fed both dogs.

"Well, this is interesting," Cherry said out loud to Hope and Joy. "I'm not used to notes all over the house. Smart, though. I'd have refed all of you. And you'd have loved it, right?" She gave both dogs another scratch and just to be sweet, got them each a treat from the cupboard.

The fancy coffee maker, looking as out of place on her worn countertop as a hen at a tea party, emitted an amazing aroma. Clay had left a mug sitting in front of the machine. It was a sweet gesture.

She poured herself a cup of coffee, then grabbed one of the scones that sat on a chipped plate in the center of her kitchen table. Eden Stratton had dropped off the goodies yesterday. She bit into it and nearly moaned with pleasure. She hadn't realized what she'd been missing by holding the neighbors at arm's length. Food deliveries, Christmas decorations, laughter, fun. It was all just a little bit scary.

Because she was enjoying it too much for her own peace of mind.

If she couldn't give Clay what he needed, if she hurt him, that would be the end of the deeper, budding friendships with the neighbors. Because she wasn't going to kid herself. If it came down to it, they'd take his side—if there were sides to be taken. Shaking off those thoughts, she finished her coffee and put the cup in the sink.

She donned her pinched-front brown hat in case it started snowing again, grabbed her scarf and coat, and after admonishing both dogs to behave themselves, headed to the barn. Normally she would have let Hope come with her. The Lab loved trotting along beside her when she took Queenie out. But it was too cold for Joy, and Hope made a great pet sitter.

The cold air bit her cheeks, making her exhale visible. The smell of cattle and horses hung heavy in the moist morning air. She looked out across the ranch. The land was flat and dotted with lodgepole pine and aspen. Deciduous hardwoods stood like skeletons across the prairie while fluffy Douglas fir framed the perimeter of the barn, their boughs heavy with lingering snow. With all the decorating that had gone on around here, it was a wonder Clay and the neighbors hadn't strung lights in all those trees, as well.

It was a beautiful piece of land. And it was hers—thanks to Uncle Ozzie and Aunt Vanessa. Oh, sure, she'd had to take out a small loan against the house when things had gotten bad before Dell had passed, but if she kept her budget tight and market prices on beef remained steady, she should be able to pay that down in the next few years.

She'd always gotten a great sense of pride riding across the property, caring for her herd, breeding her bulls and watching anxiously for the spring calves. Even the years she'd held her family and her uncle at arm's length because she'd had so much trouble keeping up, the years she'd been so fearful she'd fail with the ranch that had been gifted to her, she'd still felt so fortunate every time she looked around. If she could, she'd open her arms wide and hug the very atmosphere around her.

As soon as she entered the barn, Queenie bobbed her head over the stall door, her ears twitching. She passed several empty stalls and realized that the horses she'd been boarding were still over at the Callahan and Sons ranch. Although Clay insisted he wouldn't take any money, and the contracts she had with the owners still stood as before, Cherry didn't feel right about him housing and feeding those animals. She was up and around now. She ought to get those horses back here.

There were a couple more additions in the barn that she noticed. A fancy ATV with a flatbed attached and a brand-new Polaris snowmobile were parked next to her own little quad and aging Yamaha.

She debated which mode of transportation would be the most comfortable to catch up on her ranch happenings and opted for Queenie.

"Hey, girl. Feel like getting a little exercise?" She scratched Queenie's cheek, her forehead, then opened the stall door and went in, grabbing the curry comb to give the bay mare's light red coat some love and grooming. The stall had a fresh layer of hay and a full feed bucket.

Clay had been busy this morning for sure—as he had been every morning, she imagined, since Casanova had collided with her.

She wondered where he was. Although she wasn't sure if she was ready to see him just yet. She felt a little shy after their love making. Something she'd need to get over, for sure, because she certainly couldn't avoid him.

A couple of chickens strutted down the center aisle of the barn, clucking and pecking. She usually opened the door of the coop to let them out, but it appeared Clay had beat her to it.

She felt a weird pang, as though she'd suddenly become obsolete. This was her ranch and she was used to doing stuff. She had a system. Granted, she'd been cooped up in the house these past nine days and her system had been altered. But still… Was she really feeling jealous that Clay was taking care of her animals? Is that what was going on here?

After brushing Queenie, she began to tack her up. Raising her arms to get the bridle over the mare's ears sent her ribs screaming despite the tight corset squeezing her torso. The saddle blanket was harder. Queenie knew to drop her head for the bridle, but hoisting a blanket over a horse who stood fifteen hands was much more of a stretch, and that stretch was painful. She leaned against Queenie's warm side, breathing heavily, feeling as weak as a newborn kitten.

"We can do this, dang it. I've been saddling horses since I was ten." Stubbornness had her grabbing the saddle from its stand. The moan that escaped was unavoidable.

"Hey," Clay admonished, coming up behind her. "What the hell are you doing?"

She jumped because she hadn't heard him come in. "I'm going stir crazy inside and felt like a ride."

"You've got no business hoisting saddles—or even being on a horse for that matter." He stepped in front of her, took the saddle out of her hands and settled it on the stand, then started to remove Queenie's bridle.

"Don't you dare," she snapped, surprising herself. "I don't need you to tell me what I can and cannot do on my own ranch and with my own horses. And stop sneaking around for crying out loud. You nearly scared me half to death."

He turned at the sudden bite in her tone and frowned

when she took an involuntary step back. Darn it, why did she do that? Anger at herself and the whole situation made her bristle. Her actions were unreasonable, but she was helpless to stop them.

He studied her for a long moment, then straightened, and tugged at his hat. "Sorry. I can be a little bossy, but my intentions are good."

His sincere apology took the starch right out of her garters. And her Southern sensibilities were appalled at her ungrateful, skittish behavior. "I guess I can be a little touchy."

"See there, even more we have in common. We're both flawed."

He said it so happily she laughed. How did he do that to her? "You're something else, Clay Callahan."

"I'm hoping that's a good 'something else.'" He leaned in and pressed a gentle kiss to her lips. "I like it when you laugh."

Before she could object or even decide how she felt about the easy intimacy, he tucked his gloves in his pocket and took a step toward the saddle stand. He hesitated before actually lifting it again.

"Ginger has been asking for a nice ride. Why don't you let me saddle up your girl and mine and we can go together?"

Darn man. Did he know that kindness was her Achilles heel? The fact that he *heard* her, was now *asking* if he could tack up the horse, made her heart melt. That was happening more often that she was comfortable with.

"I didn't realize you had Ginger here."

"The day you got hurt, I was on horseback, remember? I put her away in your barn and decided to keep her here."

Since she'd been in a haze of pain medication, then a whirlwind of visitors and social activity since the accident, she hadn't really paid much attention to the logistics of Clay's daily activities. She'd only known from him telling her that her ranch was humming along as usual. And, of course, his family had been coming and going and delivering everything from food to vehicles.

"Makes sense. And she's certainly welcome."

He smiled. "Sure you want to ride the horses? I know you want to get out but we can take the ATV or snowmobile."

"I'd like to check on Casanova and he's not crazy about the noise of the equipment. Besides, I imagine Queenie will enjoy some exercise. Unless you've been riding her?" She realized she didn't know what all he'd been doing.

"No. I've turned her out each day so she's not cooped up in the barn, but I've been doing the minimum."

Because he'd been concentrating on taking care of *her*, she realized. This man. It was truly getting harder and harder to resist him.

Since she'd given him the go-ahead, he saddled the horses, then helped her mount. "You going to be warm enough?" He eyed her sheepskin-lined denim coat and blue wool scarf.

She nearly rolled her eyes. This wasn't her heaviest coat, but it was the least cumbersome. Normally she opted for the lighter garments, knowing she'd work up a sweat. She doubted she'd be doing much sweating today—at least not from exertion if Clay had anything to say about it. She might be sorry she didn't opt for her heaviest coat. "I'm fine, Clay. Don't fuss."

"Hard not to when I can clearly see you wince every time that horse takes a step."

She smiled and gave Queenie a nudge with the heel of her boot once they'd cleared the barn, determined to prove she was tougher than she looked. Well-trained, the mare broke into a trot. Cherry immediately knew she'd made a mistake.

Stubbornness would be the death of her. Her ribs howled and her calf rubbed against Queenie's side, feeling as though the stitches were surely about to pop. She pulled up on the reins.

Clay, to his credit, brought Ginger up next to her, but didn't say a word. Smart man.

Walking at this pace would take them half the day to reach the bull's pen. She should have agreed to take the quad.

"Nice day for a slow trail ride," Clay commented.

"Are you trying to make me feel better?"

"I'm sure I don't know what you mean."

"Yes, you do. I'm stubborn and you're dying to say 'I told you so.'"

"That wouldn't be very gentlemanly of me." He tipped his hat slightly and gave her a wicked grin.

"I want to check on Casanova, but I'll admit, I probably rushed things."

"We can go home."

"I know. But let's give it a try, okay?"

"Anything for you, Sugar." He held his reins easily, kept Ginger at a slow walking pace right next to Queenie.

"Are you always this agreeable?"

"Hell no," he said with a laugh. "You're special, though."

"About that…"

"Now, don't be going back on your word." He seemed to know exactly what her objection was about to be. "You agreed to give us a try."

With her body, yes. She hadn't actually said the words. But openly talking about last night made her feel shy. "I'm not sure where you intend for us to go."

"For now, just to the bullpen. From there, we'll play it by ear."

Who was this man and where had he been all her life? And

how could she trust his suave behavior? Everyone knew couples were on their best behavior in the beginning stages of a relationship. It was when the newness wore off that a person's true colors often reared up. And not always in a good way. It was so easy to get sucked in, tied down, and then, *wham*....

She didn't want to believe that Clay had a dark side. But how could she be sure? She knew firsthand how companionship and desire could turn ugly. One never started off in a relationship thinking their love would become so controlling you couldn't even go to the store without accusations and the third degree over who you saw or talked to.

When they arrived at the bullpens, her trained eye took in everything at once. Snow stuck to the ground in slushy patches. Flakes of hay were strewn over the enclosures and Casanova was munching happily. He raised his huge black head and looked at her.

"Stay put," Clay said, as he dismounted, then came around to help her down.

She raised a brow at him.

"Don't look at me in that tone of voice. There's no sense in you putting more stress on your leg when I've got perfectly fine muscles going to waste."

She laughed, something she was doing a lot of lately. "Well, we can't have that. Thank you." She let him help her off the horse and went to stand by the fence, but didn't enter the pen. She could see from here that there was no need to go in. The water in the trough wasn't iced over, and there was plenty of food to forage on the ground. Casanova looked healthy and content. Delilah, his goat companion, stood close by his side, chewing a mouthful of hay.

"Looks like he's doing good."

"Wyatt had Lyle come out."

"I know he said he was going to ask. What did Lyle say?"

"Said your boy here checked out just fine."

"I knew he would. I told you what happened was a fluke." She glanced around at the other bulls. The three younger ones were each sectioned off in their own fenced pastures. Casanova wasn't one to fight, but she surely didn't want to take a chance on injuries. Some ranchers turned the bulls out with the cows and left them year-round. Cherry preferred to keep them separate so she could time the new calves that would drop. This year, that should happen at the end of January.

Her gaze settled on Casanova as the old guy came lumbering over to the fence, his goat trotting along behind. She reached through the heavy wire to give him a scratch.

"I've never seen anyone treat this sort of animal like you do. For that matter, I've never seen a bull so anxious for petting."

"That's because you're a horse guy. Cows are super affectionate and curious. Besides, Casanova and I have been through a lot together. I think he understands me." She'd given away pieces of herself all throughout her marriage. She'd even given away a piece of Casanova to survive. She almost felt as though she needed to apologize to him for that, for not keeping him safe.

Not that he was in any danger from Wyatt. It was just that he was her responsibility. She'd entered into a pact with him —as she'd done with all of her animals—to keep him safe and healthy. And all hers. Selling off a part interest in him had been a big blow to her.

As though reading her mind, Clay asked, "It really bothers you that Wyatt owns part of this bull?"

"Yes. I know people make business deals every day, but that was a hard one for me. Casanova was all mine. He wasn't given to me to barter with."

"It's not like you've given your child away."

She shrugged. "Feels like it. I know it sounds silly to you, and I can't really articulate how I feel. It just is. He was all mine, and now he's not. And I don't want him to think it's in any way his fault."

He put his arm around her, drew her close to his side. "That's one of the things I love about you. You make everyone think you're such a tough cookie, but you're a marshmallow on the inside. You're a savvy ranch woman who rides herd with the men, but the only ones who get to see the real you are the strays you take in."

One of the things I love about you.

She knew it was a simple conversational statement. He didn't mean it in the literal sense. But it gave her a jolt none-theless.

"I think I'm getting better at letting people in. I mean, I haven't had much choice lately."

"Too bad we all had to wait for you to get injured to let your guard down."

His words slammed into her. And not in a good way. "Is that what everyone thinks of me? That I'm prickly and have my guard up?"

"You don't make it easy to know you, Sugar."

"I'm not stuck up!"

"Cherry—"

She wasn't thinking. Having it verbalized that she was indeed being judged by the folks in town took over her entire thought process, made her a little crazy. "All it would take is me getting too friendly with one of those neighbors, and I'd end up in the hospital with a busted nose! I *couldn't*—" She stopped, her eyes widening, her breath coming in fast pants.

Ohmygoshohmygoshohmygosh. What the hell am I thinking? I can't believe I blurted that out.

"Aww, sweetheart." There was a flat rock outside the pen. Clay steered her to it and urged her to sit, sat next to her, pulled her against him, and just held her. The horses followed, creating a small measure of warmth around them.

Cherry tucked her scarf more snuggly around her neck, over her chin. She was used to the weather, but she felt extra cold. Probably because of the direction of her thoughts, the bald words that had slipped out. She wanted to call them back but couldn't. Her outburst, the feeling of being out of control, of being out of her body, was settling a bit. Nothing she could do about it now. The words were out.

"I think you're going to have to tell me about that, Sugar. I know you like to guard your privacy but it's just me here. And I think you need to tell someone who won't judge you."

"Why do you think I'd worry about you judging *me?*" Never mind that's exactly what had caused her outburst. "Dell was the one with the nasty temper."

"Because of your actions. If you were just concerned with what we all thought about Dell, I don't think we'd be having this same conversation."

She turned her head and looked at him, at the concern on his handsome features, the banked anger in his gaze. "How do you know you won't change your opinion of me?"

"I've got plenty of my own baggage. I'm not about to criticize someone else's. Besides, I suspect I know a little of what you went through. My mind is conjuring some pretty nasty stuff, so it would probably be kinder on your part to tell me the real story so I can relax."

And just like that, in the blink of an eye, he made her smile. She wasn't sure how he could even get that emotion out of her with the way her insides were trembling. Clay was a special man.

"There's nothing relaxing about my story. Something happened to Dell when he drank. He tended to bouts of depression, to feel like his life didn't matter. I'm not sure if the depression caused the alcohol dependency or if the alcohol caused the depression. And I could never pinpoint whether his moodiness was seasonal or not. Sometimes I thought that he got worse during rodeo season—because he could no longer compete. His rodeo days were his glory days. He was famous in those circles, and when he stopped riding, everyone forgot who he was."

"He still liked to talk about 'the good old days'," Clay said.

"Yes. Sometimes I was embarrassed for him. It got a little pathetic."

"Why did you stay?"

She snorted. "Well, that's the sixty-four-thousand-dollar question, isn't it?"

He fingered the ends of her hair, placed a barely discernable kiss on her temple, didn't push.

She signed. "I'm not one hundred percent sure why I stayed, and that's the shame that I bear."

"Oh, no, Sugar. You have nothing to be ashamed of. What Dell put you through was not your fault."

"I was embarrassed. And frankly, the first time he hit me, I was flat out stunned. It was right after we got here to Shotgun Ridge. We'd already been married nearly ten years, and he'd been a moody asshole at times but nothing like that. I didn't want to tell Mama and Daddy or Uncle Ozzie. I kept thinking things were going to get better. That it was a fluke. Then, I guess I kind of got stuck. I kept rationalizing and excusing away the behavior. The land was mine. The house was mine. I had the animals to think about. How could I abandon them? Dell wasn't about to leave, so I was stuck."

"You could have come to us. To Cheyenne. He'd have arrested his ass. Given you a restraining order."

"That's all very rational sounding in hindsight, Clay. But I wasn't thinking clearly. I was scared. Dell said some awful things in his fits of rage, made vile threats. I couldn't trust him not to follow through, not to hurt one of the animals or someone in my family. I thought I could control him. Cajole him out of his moods. It wasn't as if it was an everyday occurrence. So, I retreated—from my family and from everyone else, kept to myself and tried to keep the peace. Before I knew it, I was in too deep. I'd lost myself."

"I wish I'd have followed through and stopped by here more often."

"You'd have made things worse for me."

A muscle in his jaw ticked and his hand fisted on his thigh. All tell-tell signs of anger. Signs she was conditioned to notice and react to. Hardly aware, she shifted away from him.

"He couldn't have stood up to the whole town, and that's what it would have come to had we known."

"But I didn't know that, Clay. I never started out as a little girl thinking someone would hurt me. In my fantasies, I was the princess in the castle and my knight worshiped me. I was bossy and strong-willed and fun. I thought I had great intuition when it came to judging a person's character. Marriage to Dell showed me how very wrong I was. So, now where do I go from here? How can I ever trust my own judgment again? Especially about a man? A relationship?"

"Even me?" Clay asked, incredulous. "Are you lumping *me* in the same category as Dell?"

She didn't know where to go with this conversation. "I do trust you, Clay. As much as I'm capable of. I know in my heart that you're a good guy. It's just that anger or discord sends me into a spiral. Not just with you. I can't explain it. Maybe it's an irrational fear, but it's real to me."

He cupped her cheek. Although his eyes were hard, his touch was gentle.

"Like now," she said. "You're angry."

"Not with you." She had an idea he really wanted to shout but was making every effort to calm down. "I'm angry that Dell's dead, and I can't beat the shit out of him. I'm angry that he put you through hell. I'm angry that I didn't act on my own suspicions and intervene."

"You suspected?"

"I wondered because you were so skittish, as though you were afraid to have a conversation with any of the neighbors. That was when he was alive. I suspected after the accident when I saw the bruise on your cheek. I figured it could have been from the accident, but a nagging voice inside me kept poking. It didn't sit right with me. So, what happened that day of the accident?"

"He was drunk."

"Why'd you get in the car with him?"

She raised her brows, gave him a self-deprecating look. "He would have made a scene. We were parked in front of Brewers. I didn't want anyone to know things were amiss."

"And why were they amiss?"

"Dell didn't need a special reason. But that particular day, he'd been drinking his lunch at Brewers—on top of the three beers he'd downed before we'd even gone to town. That was pretty out of character for him—drinking in public. He usually binged in private, guarded his secret. I managed to get him out of Brewers before he caused a scene, but I needed to go over to Jenkins Feed before we went home. I wasn't thinking clearly, I guess. I was trying to make conversation and placate him out of his surliness, pretending everything was sunshine and roses when my heart was actually galloping like a horse with a bee under the saddle blanket. I sort of wondered out loud if we should try a different kind of feed for the herd. But I made the mistake of mentioning it in Henry's store, and Henry overheard. He agreed with me. Dell clammed up and pretty much marched me out of the feed store and into the car. I knew right away I'd screwed up."

She stood, because this next part wasn't something she wanted to say while facing him. It would be a revelation of her personality that wouldn't shine a nice light on her.

"I hated Dell." There, she'd said it. "And God help me, I wished him dead. Especially that day of the accident. We were fighting in the car. Yelling. I'd finally reached the tipping point to where I didn't give a damn what happened. I told him I was sick of him, that I didn't have an ounce of feeling left for him. I should have waited until we were home instead of finally growing a spine in a moving vehicle. But I didn't care anymore. I called him pathetic. He reached across the seat and punched me."

Clay sucked in air, then swore and stood as well.

Cherry moved closer to Queenie. Just that slight move made her feel more in control. She could mount and leave at a moment's notice. She had an out. She was safe. In control.

She glanced back at Clay, told him with her body language and her features that she really didn't want him coming any closer.

He evidently got the message, because he stood where he was. He took off his hat, raked his fingers through his hair, then put it back on and tucked his hands in the front pockets of his jeans. Maybe trying to give her the impression that he was harmless.

And he probably was.

But who could ever be one hundred percent certain?

"Thankfully, it was a solo accident, so no one else was hurt."

"Except for you," Clay said quietly.

She nodded. Some of those scars she would carry for a lifetime. "The momentum of him hitting me and the lack of reflexes from the alcohol made him lose control of the truck. He overcorrected, the tires caught the lip of the road, and we flipped, ending up head-on into a telephone pole. He was too cocky to wear a seatbelt and was ejected from the car." She wrapped her arms around herself, that day so clear in her mind. She could smell the acrid scent of burning rubber, hear the scream of the tires as they tried to find purchase on asphalt, feel the percussion in her chest as the truck came to a bone-jarring, explosive stop. Then the eerie quiet of nothingness. Not a bird in the sky or car on the highway. For a moment, she'd thought she'd died and gone to heaven. The silence and stillness had been that complete.

Then she'd taken inventory of herself. She'd clearly been in shock, but she'd been amazed that she'd come through such a horrendous event with just a black eye and split lip—compliments of Dell's fist rather than the near-tragic wreck. She might have believed in the miracle of angels, that she'd been divinely snatched from the jaws of death, had it not been for her thoughts.

She didn't imagine God rewarded hatred—even on a subconscious level.

"I had a lot of time waiting for someone to come along. I knew Dell was dead. I could see that he wasn't moving."

She looked at him then, steadily. "I wasn't sad or hysterical. I was relieved. Utterly, thankfully relieved."

He took a step toward her, but she held up her hand. She needed some space. Putting her foot in the stirrup, she grabbed the saddle horn and, ignoring the screaming of her ribs, hoisted herself onto Queenie. "How awful does that make me? What kind of woman is glad when her husband is dead?"

She started to move away, but Clay stepped up, put his hand on Queenie's bridle. The other hand rested on her thigh. "Don't run away, Sugar."

"I'm feeling a fair amount of shame right now, and it's hard to face you."

"You don't need to feel that way with me." He reached for Ginger's bridle, hoisted himself into his saddle despite her anxiousness to put space between them.

"I don't know what it's going to take to convince you that you're the most amazing, kind, loving woman around, but I'm going to try to figure it out. Because you deserve so much better than you've gotten so far in life."

"Clay—"

"Nope. We're done with this conversation."

He took her hand, leaned in so he could place a sweet kiss on her knuckles. Tears sprang to her eyes.

"Thank you for trusting me with your secrets," he said softly.

"I didn't mean to," she admitted.

"I know. But you did, and that's progress. Now, we're

going to figure out how to bury that past where it belongs. Starting with the ride back to the ranch. Just you and me, Sugar, and these horses."

Cherry felt raw. She'd give anything to do just that—bury the past. But it was so deeply imbedded in her subconscious, she wasn't sure it was even possible.

CHAPTER 8

*C*lay pulled out his cell phone and made a call on the way back to Cherry's barn. He'd always thought it looked ridiculous to talk on a phone while on a horse, but these were extenuating circumstances.

"Why are you asking Abbe to make us food?" Cherry asked, dropping gingerly to the ground and leading Queenie into her stall. She was definitely limping more than when they'd left.

Clay followed, reaching for her saddle before she could. "Because it'll be dark soon, and I have a plan."

"I think there's soup in the house." She slid the blanket off Queenie and folded it.

"We're not staying in tonight."

"No?"

"Nope. I've decided we need to do something fun. Something that has nothing to do with ranching or work." This woman had had way too little enjoyment in her life lately and he wanted to be the man to fix that. He flicked the switch in the barn to turn on the electricity to the Christmas lights.

"Isn't it a little early for that?"

"A little. Come on, let's go." He steered her toward his truck.

"Where?" She balked slightly, but he kept up a gentle pressure.

"It's a surprise. You'll know soon enough."

She got in the truck. "Shouldn't we feed the pets?"

"We won't be long. And it won't hurt them to have a late supper." He jogged around the front of the truck and joined her. "Just sit back and let me be in charge of your entertainment tonight."

"I'm not super big on surprises—or letting someone else be in the driver's seat."

"I'm guessing you'll want me in this particular driver's seat. Relax for a few minutes. Let me take care of you."

He drove them over to the Callahan and Son's farm and stopped in front of the hangar. Clay grinned when he saw Abbe and Grant standing next to the Bell Ranger helicopter, which Grant had helpfully moved outside for them. Abbe's little girl, Jolene, danced around, tossing a stick for her tiny Maltese, Harley.

"That puppy doesn't seem to know he's little," Cherry noted. "I bet Joy would have a ball with him."

"You're probably right." He got out of the truck and came around to help her out. "We should arrange a doggie playdate for them."

Cherry laughed, and Clay felt like he'd done his job—and he'd hardly begun. He wanted this to be a light evening. No ghosts or hard conversations or reminders of the past. Just fun and the beauty of the season.

"Is that helicopter sitting outside for some significant reason?"

"I thought we'd take a flight and see the Christmas lights from the air. It's a pretty amazing sight." He turned to his brother, then couldn't help himself and peeked beneath the blanket to the sleeping baby in Grant's arms. Little Faith Callahan was five months old, and together with her sister, Jolene, had her daddy wrapped around her baby finger.

"Thanks for getting the bird out."

"No problem. I just wish I'd thought of this first. Now you're showing me up in the date department."

Clay grinned and looked at Abbe. "He slackin' already on romance?"

Abbe, who stood nearly six feet in her boots, looked up at her husband with such a soft expression on her face, Clay was sure he could feel her love sizzle all the way over here. "He does just fine, thank you very much." Abbe had the same Texas accent as Cherry—just not as strong. "I fixed y'all some turkey croissants, and there's a thermos of soup. Nothing fancy, but I'm no gourmet cook like Eden and you didn't give me much time."

"I'm sure it'll be delicious," Cherry said. "I didn't mean for him to impose. I could have packed soup." She looked at Clay. "*If* someone had told me what we were doing."

"No imposition," Abbe assured her. "In fact, I'm tickled that Clay thought of this. Now I'm going to insist we get our turn in this whirly-bird tomorrow. Jolie will get a kick out of lookin' at lights this way. How are you doing, by the way?" she asked, glancing at Cherry's leg.

"Healing."

"Putting up a brave front," Clay added, answering more truthfully than she would. "Thanks, you guys. We won't be long—we'll need to get home early to feed the menagerie of pets."

"Call Wyatt," Grant suggested. "He'll run over and handle it."

"No," Cherry said quickly. "They'll be fine. No sense in anyone else doing more than they already are for me."

Clay put his arm around her shoulders, steered her toward the helicopter. "You know you're being a killjoy. Little Ian Malone would probably pay you to let him come play with those dogs."

"Yes, well, I'm sure little Ian has plenty of his own animals to feed." She nodded her head toward the helicopter. "You can fly this thing?"

"You don't sound very confident," he said with a laugh. "But yes, I've got well over a hundred flight hours. Ethan and I couldn't let Grant show us up. When he came back from the service and bought this beauty, we were determined he wouldn't be the only one piloting it. Just didn't seem fair."

He helped her into the cockpit and handed her a set of headphones. She put them on, then fumbled with the seatbelt and safety harness.

"Need some help?"

She jumped when the sound of his voice floated through the headphones. She glanced at him and smiled. "Little different than tacking up a pony, but I think I got it. Can you hear me? Or do I need to press something for us to talk?"

"We're tuned to the same frequency, so I can hear you fine. It's going to get noisy in here, though. Ever been up in a helicopter before?"

"No. This is a first."

He grinned. "I like being your first."

Oh, how she wished he *had* been. How her life might have been so different.

The rotors began to turn, whipping the air, and excitement built.

"I checked the weather. No snow tonight, so we should have a clear view. Ready to go look at Christmas lights?"

She nodded. This was the craziest thing. As a girl, the whole family had piled into the car and gone driving through the countryside and neighborhoods looking at the festive Christmas decorations and lights. She'd never thought she'd be doing something like that in a helicopter.

Their shoulders brushed as he used both hands and feet on the various controls and sticks to put the bird in the air. It appeared there was a lot more to flying a helicopter than an airplane. Her stomach pitched as the skids left the ground, as they hovered then slowly turned and climbed, circling over the ranch house and heading off into the night sky. She watched him, admitted she was a little turned on by his attention and skill flying the aircraft.

Was there anything this man couldn't do?

Through the glass windshield and sides, she had a clear view of the entire Shotgun Ridge valley. They flew over her ranch and Wyatt's. She could see Casanova below in his pen as Clay activated a spotlight, turning the white snow into a sparkling blanket beneath them.

"Look. Delilah is on Casanova's back."

Clay glanced at her and smiled. He loved hearing the excitement in her voice. Especially after what she'd told him this afternoon. My God, how had she endured such a marriage? And why would she think that made her any less?

He wanted to spend the rest of his life making up for the awful time she'd had in her worthless marriage. He just wasn't sure she would let him. There was something she was still worried about, something causing her to hold back.

At least he could give her this. A few hours of sightseeing. A few hours were there were no responsibilities or expectations. Only beauty and wonder.

As they flew over the town, he brought the helicopter low, keeping the craft at a safe distance, but giving her the full effect of seeing the twenty-foot Christmas tree in the town's square from the air. It was a sight to behold, for sure.

The star at the tiptop of the tree twinkled as though a halo surrounded it.

Miracles had been known to happen in Shotgun Ridge. Especially at Christmastime.

Clay was counting on it being his turn this year. His and Cherry's.

~

BY THE TIME they got home, Cherry's emotions are all over the place. She'd unburdened her soul to Clay this afternoon, and although she'd expected the sky to fall, it hadn't. Instead, he'd taken her up into that sky, showed her the world from the vantage point of his helicopter's cockpit. Not your everyday date.

Not your everyday man, either.

It felt like he was offering her the world on a platter. Although she might be getting ahead of herself here. He hadn't actually made any verbal offers. And if he did, what would she do? Was it even possible to let go after the type of trauma she'd lived through? To forgive and forget and believe that the world was a perfect place and everyone in it had the best of intentions? That life with Clay would remain exactly as it had these last nine magical days?

Melodramatic thoughts for sure. But her fears were real.

They simmered just below the surface, waiting to blindside her when she least expected it. That was getting plenty old for her. It would surely begin to wear on a partner as well.

While Clay was out checking the horses, she let Joy and Hope out the kitchen door, and smiled when they hurried through their business and raced back in the house.

"Cold, hmm babies? Or are you just starving half to death?" She dished out a late-night meal and they nearly collided with each other to get at the food. That made her feel a little guilty for making the poor things wait so long to eat.

It was interesting how she and Clay had fallen into a routine of divvying up the chores—when he would even let her do anything, that was. He insisted on taking care of all things outdoors. But he wanted to run the show indoors as well. She practically had to race him for the can opener to feed the dogs. You'd think her hands were injured rather than her leg. Each day she tested a little more weight on her leg and although there was a good bit of soreness, she could have gotten by on her own. The stitches were dissolving and the herbal poultice had sped up the healing considerably.

So why was she still accepting Clay's presence in her home?

The old Cherry would have kicked him out by now, sent him home to his own ranch and muscled through her lingering pain to get things done. Alone.

Instead, she continued to let him make her life easier. The truth was, she enjoyed having him here. She loved his smile, the way he cuddled the puppy and wrestled with Hope. His gentle touch on the kitten's fur—and on her own cheek. She loved his quiet presence in the house.

And she loved sleeping with him—not just the non-sleeping parts, but the closeness. He was giving her glimpses of what could be.

She shouldn't be indulging in this yearning, because what *could* be and what *would* be were two different things. Her leg would heal. Clay would go home. Life would return to the way it was.

The fact remained that she still didn't believe she was the right woman for him.

But was it so wrong to want a few more days before reality set in?

When the dogs had finished eating, she grabbed a squeaky toy and tossed it for Joy, thinking she needed to expend some pent-up puppy energy before bed. Joy didn't seem interested, just plopped down instead of giving chase.

"That's a first," Clay said, coming in behind her and causing her to jump.

"Hmm. Might want to have a walk through the house and see if this little one has been up to mischief. She clearly did something to tire herself out."

He smiled and gave the puppy a scratch.

Cherry suddenly felt shy. The animals were settled for the night. She and Clay were alone in the house. The lights twinkled on the Christmas tree. A fire burned in the hearth, the warmth even more welcome after being out in the cold night.

So, what was next? Should they sit here and talk?

What she wanted to do was take him by the hand and lead him to the bedroom.

"You're thinking awfully loud." Clay came up to her, gently pushed her hair behind her ear, placed a lingering kiss just below her jaw.

Her heartbeat leaped. "I had a good time tonight. Thank you."

He lowered his mouth to hers, kissed her with that gentleness she'd come to crave. "You're welcome," he murmured against her lips. "Tired?"

She threaded her fingers through his hair. Every nerve ending in her body was now standing at full attention.

"Not *that* tired." It had been a good many years since she'd flirted. She was rusty at it, but it felt good. Empowering. "I wouldn't object to having a bed beneath us, though."

"Us?"

"Yes. Us."

And that's all she needed to say. The world tilted as he lifted her in his arms and carried her down the hall. He made her feel tiny and cherished, both fairly foreign emotions in her life until now. Her body made a slow, sensuous slide down the front of his as he lowered her, inch by exquisite inch, to her feet. His hands never leaving her, he lifted her shirt and pulled it over her head.

"Mmm. I wondered what was so stiff under here." He studied the corset that hugged her torso. "How'd you get this on by yourself? There has to be twenty little hooks."

"It wasn't easy. But I'll be ever so grateful if you'll please get me out of it."

"My pleasure." He unhooked the garment slowly. "Sexiest rib-brace I've ever seen." As he uncovered her skin, he leaned in and ran his lips over the creases the tight garment had caused. "Hurt?" he asked.

"No." All she could feel was desire. And he wasn't moving nearly fast enough for her. She pulled him up to her, initiated a kiss that sent a wildfire bolt of heat through her. She couldn't get enough fast enough. She tore at his shirt, pulling it over his head, reached for the snap of his jeans.

He stopped and looked at her, his gaze intense, his touch

determined. He was a man who knew what he wanted and wasn't about to apologize for it.

It was the most utterly thrilling look any man had ever given her. It made her feel beautiful and sexy and gave her a measure of confidence she'd been sorely lacking.

Without breaking eye contact, he undressed her, then dropped to his knees in front of her, his gaze a fiery caress. "You are so damned beautiful."

His voice held a reverence that banished any shyness she might have felt. His lips gently caressed her ribs, as though he could heal her with his mouth alone.

"Clay..." His gentleness was too much. She'd never felt so cherished.

"I know." He stood and lowered her to the bed, followed her and fitted his body to hers, making sure his weight wasn't too much for her healing injuries. He used his knee to nudge her legs apart. "Put your legs around me."

"But...you're still dressed."

"Trust me."

She did as he asked, felt the exquisite friction of denim against silk as he pressed against her. His hands beneath her hips lifted her higher, harder against him.

Cherry wasn't certain how much of this teasing she could take. She felt a scream building inside her, wanted to rush, wanted completion. Her hands danced over the muscled contours of his back and shoulders as she strained against him.

But he wouldn't be hurried.

With a single fingertip, he traced a path from the center of her breastbone to her navel. He watched her, smiled when she shivered, then slid his palm between her legs and cupped her.

Chills raced over her skin. Chills of desire the likes of

which she'd never felt before. He was a man in every sense of the word, strong and capable with a masculinity and sexuality hot enough to burn and cool enough to surprise. An absolute magician when he put his hands on her.

She wanted to participate, but she was swept up in sensation, as though paralyzed by the exquisite desire his touch created.

"Clay…"

"This time's for you." With his lips, tongue, and body, he tasted and touched every inch of her, wrapping her in a cocoon of sensation, of discovery; aroused her to the point of the most pleasurable pain. Slipping her yellow silk panties down her legs, he kissed her in the most intimate way a man can kiss a woman.

She gripped the sheets, dug her heels into the mattress. The instant flash of uncertainty, of objection, died in her throat. Sensation upon sensation rolled over her. It was too much. And not nearly enough. The orgasm that ripped through her stole her breath and her reason. Nothing existed at that moment except Clay. He'd just taken her to heights she'd only ever dreamed about.

She'd thought she was experienced.

How very wrong she'd been.

Needing more, greedy for more, she gripped his shoulders, urged him up her body, kissed him with all the desire and strength she had in her. "Now, Clay." She tore at his jeans, urging him to be one with her. She managed to get the zipper down, shoved her hand inside, and closed her fingers around the steel-hard length of him.

"Sugar…wait."

"No way." She rolled with him, fitted her body on top of his, felt the fire and friction of skin to skin, hard to soft. She kissed his neck, his chest, reveled in his strength as he cupped her behind, pressed, rocked her against his straining erection. Taking her by surprise, he rolled with her, swept her beneath him.

"Hey. I wasn't done," she said.

"Neither am I." And he preceded to make good on his vow that this was for her. Where before their movements were fevered, now they were gentle. As was his kiss. He kissed her as though he wanted to absorb her right into his very soul.

And then he entered her, filled her so full she couldn't tell where one began and the other ended. Slowly, oh, so slowly, he slid in and out, holding his weight off of her, his gaze never wavering from hers. He watched her, worshiped her.

Made love to her.

Sensations built, washed over her in wave after exquisite wave of ecstasy. With increasing tempo, he made love to her mind, body, and soul. He focused his entire being on her pleasure alone. She could see it in his eyes, feel it in his every move, taste it on his lips.

He took her on the ride of her life, flying on the wings of desire so hot it scorched her from the inside out, healed her, changed her life.

And like a rushing whirlwind sweeping her along without a will, she shattered around him, rode the crest of bliss as she felt him reach his own peak.

It was a joining that had touched her soul and laid her emotions bare.

Clay Callahan had satisfied a physical craving, yet had created an emotional yearning in her that could only spell danger—especially to her need for control.

But she was terribly afraid that her body and emotions were about to betray her. Because if she wasn't mistaken, the final piece of a sweet and complicated puzzle had just clicked into place, bringing with it the swift and utter feelings of love.

And that was a disaster, because she'd promised herself, written it in her own blood, that she'd never again succumb to the kind of strong emotions that could cause a person to surrender to another.

CHAPTER 9

"It smells good in here," Clay said.

"Mmm." She ought to be used to the *morning after* shyness by now, but she still experienced a jolt of unease, albeit a slight one. "Gingerbread men and sugar cookies. Mama used to bake them every year when Brooke and I were little."

"Having grown up in a house full of men, I don't have homey cookie memories. But these smell pretty amazing." He reached around her and snagged a sugar cookie that was cooling on a wire rack. "Have you talked to your family lately?"

"Yes. Mama calls once a week. I hadn't realized how much I'd missed talking to her until after Dell died."

"You didn't talk to your mom during your marriage?" He leaned against the counter, crossed his booted ankles.

"Not often." She squeezed white icing from a baker's cone and outlined each of the cooled gingerbread men. Her hair fell forward, shielding her from Clay's view.

"Why don't I fly you home for Christmas? We can take

135

Abbe's twin engine Baron. It's a faster plane than the ones my brothers and I own."

"Good night, how many planes do y'all have?"

"Three, counting Abbe's. Since she's married to Grant, we've claimed possession. Plus the Ranger."

She shook her head, almost tempted to take him up on the offer. "Mama already asked me to come out and I told her I was staying home. Besides, you don't want to be away from your family this close to the holiday."

"I'm happiest wherever you are."

The white bead of icing squiggled. When he said things like that she wanted to melt.

But she didn't want him organizing her life. It was getting more difficult by the day to keep from letting him take over—especially after the life-altering time they'd spent in bed. And her fears over actually falling in love.

Besides, she'd already made up her mind to stay home. Maybe she was being unreasonably stubborn, but she wasn't ready to face her family—at least not on the spur of the moment, not without a whole lot more preparation.

Her parents and sister assumed she was the strong one, and although she believed she was on the road to becoming the woman she'd once been—and Clay was playing a big part in that—she wasn't quite there yet. Until then, until she could trust herself not to crumble at the first sight of her mama or sister, she needed to stay right where she was. Besides, she had a responsibility here—to the ranch and to the animals and to her bottom line.

I'm happiest where you are. Lord, he was tempting.

"I need to be here. This ranch was a gift. It was entrusted to me, as were these innocent animals. My main goal is to build this herd and stay above water financially. One day, I'd like to not have to worry about the cost of feed or fuel. I'll get there because I'm not afraid of hard work, but meanwhile—"

"Of course, you will. But is that what's keeping you from going home? Your own measure of success or lack of it?"

Was it? "Maybe a little bit." She pressed the cookie cutter into the gingerbread dough, then carefully transferred the happy little shapes to the baking sheet. "Mama still thinks I'm grieving." She glanced up quickly, then back to what she was doing.

"Maybe you are."

She snorted. "I seem to recall airing all my dirty laundry with you."

"Grief doesn't have to be for a person. Maybe you're grieving the idea of the life you always wanted."

"Be kind of silly to hold onto little girl dreams at my age."

But was she? Could she?

∽

CLAY SPENT the rest of the morning repairing a section of fence the cows had trampled on the border of Cherry and Wyatt's property. He'd practically had to sneak out while she was busy baking cookies. Otherwise, she'd have given him grief. Cherry Peyton did not accept help from others easily. Even though he'd been here nearly two weeks, she still gave him a hard time over trying to help her.

When he came back inside, lingering heat from the oven stung his cold cheeks. The kitchen was clean and cookies were stacked neatly on decorative trays. Removing his hat, he set it aside on the counter and moved to the sink to wash his hands.

"You about ready in here?" he asked.

Cherry paused, the two kittens in one arm and Joy in the other. Hope lay nicely at her feet, head on her paws, her expressive eyes shifting between the adults. "Ready for what?"

Clay grinned. Naturally, she'd have animals in her arms. He didn't blame her. They were all so darned cute.

"We're due over at Cheyenne and Emily's, remember? John White Cloud is bringing a group of kids from the reservation over for their monthly horseback rides and cookout. I volunteered us to help out."

"I'm not sure I should go," she hedged. "We've been leaving the animals a lot and—"

"Sugar." He stopped her with a finger to her lips. "The animals are fine. They've got toys and warmth and food and each other." He took the kittens from her and set them on the floor next to Hope, who nearly vibrated with happiness at having the baby fur balls climbing over her.

"You sure do have quite a social calendar." She shifted Joy in her arms, cuddling the wiggling puppy.

"*We* do."

"I'm just not used to all this socializing."

"You really don't like it?"

"I *do* like it. A lot. It's just new…and I guess my first reaction is to decline."

"Well, good thing I'm here to expand your horizons."

She smiled. "What's the plan? Are we supposed to bring something?"

"Just ourselves. Emily's got a whole two-weeks-before-Christmas thing planned for the reservation kids. They usually don't come into town on Christmas Eve for the gifts Santa leaves under the town tree, so she and Amy Lucas organized an early celebration for them this year. Some of those kids are fostered on the reservation and they've never known what it's like to ride horses or receive gifts." He glanced at the kittens who were burrowing their way under Hope's chin. Once the kittens had acclimated, it had become apparent that they were indeed older than they'd first suspected and Cherry had easily switched them to regular kitten food rather than continuing with the bottle feeding.

"Are you planning to rehome these kittens?"

"Yes. Although Hope will probably stop speaking to me."

"We could take them with us. One of the families from the reservation might be interested."

"Couldn't hurt. If we keep them in the laundry basket they'll be out of the way, but still on display."

"What about Joy?" He hated to even ask.

"No." She shook her head, her answer immediate. "This little love bug is mine."

"I was hoping you'd say that."

She kissed Joy's head, gave her another cuddle, then set her on the floor next to Hope and the kittens. "I was so mad when someone dumped her off on the highway like they did, but I'm beginning to think it was meant to be. She was meant to be mine."

And mine, he thought, but kept that to himself. She was still skittish. As much as he wanted to claim her as his family, animals and all, he still needed to tread carefully. "Definitely had an angel watching over her to end up with you. Lucky pup."

"I think I'm the lucky one."

He looked at the dogs. Joy and Hope. Interesting choice of names. And perfect for Cherry Peyton.

~

CLAY AND CHERRY had just arrived as two white vans pulled into the yard at the sheriff's ranch. John White Cloud got out of one vehicle as children spilled out the side sliding doors. John was Cheyenne Bodine's uncle and one of the elders on the reservation. The second van was driven by John's wife, Jenny.

"Looks like Stony's already here with the horses," Clay said. He pulled the laundry basket from the back seat of the truck. Tucked in with the kittens were the extras from Cherry's morning baking spree.

"What are you going to do with Kris and Jingle?"

"I'll put them over by the heaters so all the kids can get a good look. You want to take the cookies inside?"

"Looks like the food tables are set up by the barn. Might as well put them there."

"I'll handle it. Will you be okay for a few minutes while I go help Stony unload?"

"Of course. I don't need a babysitter. I'm just annoyed that I can't get over there and help with the horses."

He pressed a kiss to her forehead, and she immediately looked around to see if anyone was watching. Clay noticed. "We're not fooling anyone, you know."

Cherry sighed, shrugged. "I'm a little uncomfortable with...you know."

"Public displays of affection?" he asked with a grin. He squeezed her hand, then raised it to his lips and kissed her knuckles. "I'll try to control myself. But you don't make it easy."

She nearly fainted when he kissed her hand. It was so romantic, so unlike what she was used to, so what she *wanted* to get used to. Spellbound, she watched him jog away to help with the horses. He should have looked silly with a kitten-filled laundry basket under his arm. Instead, he looked sexy as all get out. Slim, denim-covered hips, well-worn boots, brown leather jacket, and his signature white hat. A cowboy through and through. Any minute now, she'd start to drool.

Lord, she was getting in deep.

Before she could decide whether to follow and observe what was happening outside by the corrals, or make her way into the Bodine's kitchen where she figured the rest of the women were, John White Cloud appeared beside her. She nearly gasped. He hadn't made a sound.

"Hey," she said, surprised at the breathlessness in her voice. She wasn't afraid of the older man—she hardly knew him. But he did make her a little nervous. It was his silence and the penetrating way he looked at people, as though he could read their soul.

He pulled a small tin out of his pocket. It resembled the kind of container that normally held snuff. "I am making a delivery from our medicine man, Little Joe Coyote, who is also my brother-in-law. You will put this on your ribs. It will heal the pain."

Cherry wasn't sure a salve would work on bruised ribs. And how had John or his brother-in-law even known about her injury? Probably Clay or his brothers. Or Uncle Ozzie.

John nodded as though she'd actually spoken her thoughts aloud. "You are revered in the community. Word of your injuries travels far. They have for many years."

What?

She didn't have time to question or even wonder if there was some sort of voodoo mind-reading going on because Abbe came to stand next to her. "Trust me. That stuff stinks to the high heavens, but it works like magic. Two days and you'll be good as new. Believe me, I know. I had a black eye that was a killer. I used this stuff and felt good as new."

Cherry remembered how Abbe had gotten that black eye —when the mob had kidnapped her and roughed her up. They'd also shot Grant. That had been a very bad day all around, not just for Abbe and Grant, but for the whole town. Cherry had been part of the search party when Abbe had gone missing. She didn't normally join in on socializing, but she rarely missed an event where neighbors were needed to help out—whether that be rebuilding a barn, rounding up cattle, or watching the highways for kidnappers.

She opened the lid of the tin and gave a sniff, then jerked back and wrinkled her nose.

Abbe laughed. "Told you."

Cherry figured it couldn't hurt to try it. "Thank you.," she said to John. "And please give my thanks to Little Joe Coyote." She wouldn't have minded having some of this to try when she'd had her own black eye.

And that kind of memory had no place here today.

Smoke from the barbeques rose in the air, reminding Cherry of childhood fairs, horse competitions, and family reunions. The smell of hot dogs and hamburgers wafted over the ranch as happy children rode horses with the help of several of the men. Clay was one of them.

Cherry watched him. He was so good with the children, a reinforcement that he should have kids of his own.

Snow piled on the rooftops and atop the fence posts, but that didn't deter the kids or the adults. As with her ranch, colored lights twinkled from every eave. A Douglas fir stood halfway between the house and corral, decorated with shiny balls and lights. Extension cords disguised in tubing fed electricity to the tree from the barn. Cheyenne and Emily had gone all out, placing large heaters next to the corral and the tree where they'd set up tables and chairs. Gifts wrapped in two different patterns were placed beneath the tree, blue stripes and red stripes. Cherry assumed they were to tell between boys and girls. Emily Bodine seemed to have thought of everything.

"You must go inside and warm up," John White Cloud said, making her jump. He was so quiet and still, she'd nearly forgotten he was there.

She glanced over to where Clay was helping a little boy mount a horse.

"He watches you," John said. "As he has never watched another woman. You must go inside where it is warm."

For a minute she was confused. Did he mean she should go inside so Clay wouldn't watch her?

"You have injuries that are not yet healed," the older man clarified. "Yet you wish to hide that fact from the rest of us. You should not put more on your body than is necessary. Little Joe Coyote told me this before he offered the salve. He would not presume to advise you himself." The old man suddenly grinned when he was normally so solemn. "I have no such problem. It is becoming somewhat of a habit that I am butting into others' businesses—just ask my wife. Come." He took her by the arm and steered her to the kitchen door.

What was with the older generation in this town? Her uncle and his band of matchmakers. Now the reservation elders making jokes and giving cryptic health advice—and reading minds. She was sure of it.

A blast of heat and the smell of baby and cinnamon swirled around her the minute the door was open.

Emily looked up from the stove. "Hey, neighbor. Come on in and warm up. Don't mind the mess. These twins don't know the meaning of picking up behind themselves, and I'm too tired to do it."

Cherry smiled. The twins—who couldn't be more than ten or eleven months old—were obviously too young to clean house and Emily clearly had the energy of three women, judging by the amount of food and preparations evident in the kitchen. And the number of guests milling around, both inside and out.

However, baby paraphernalia was everywhere. Two little cherubs, one boy and one girl, were in little seats with rollers, wheeling themselves around the kitchen and the chaos. There were beads and stuffed toys and activities attached to their trays, and mushed up cookies smeared over the plastic tray as well as their faces. She could see the family room from the kitchen and couldn't help but smile when she saw the Christmas tree inside of a playpen.

Cheyenne's husky, Blue, came charging through the front room, surprising Cherry. She'd never seen this dog so exuberant. The animal went everywhere with the sheriff and was the most well-behaved, well-trained dog in the county. To see him racing through the house like a wild wolf was shocking. Hot on his trail were two little munchkins—Nikki Stratton and Ian Malone, and bringing up the rear, ears flying, was Nikki's black Gordon Setter, Rosie, who appeared determined not to be left out of the fun game of chase through the house.

Cherry leaped back as both kids skidded to a halt an instant before they mowed her down.

"Sorry!" they chimed in unison, then took off again.

"You kids stop running through the house!" Dora Callahan yelled, coming out of one of the bedrooms holding a baby boy in one arm and a diaper in the other. "The sheriff is going to arrest you and throw you in the jailhouse."

Both kids halted again, this time in the kitchen and only long enough to accept a cookie from the tray Emily Bodine held out to them. "Will we really get arrested?" Nikki asked Emily. "You married him. You could tell him not to, right?"

"Well, I imagine I could pull a few strings. But only if you mind your moms, okay?"

It had been Dora Callahan who'd admonished them to use their inside manners, not their own moms. Cherry decided there was sort of a sister wives thing going on with regard to all these kids.

"Okay. Can we go ride the horses now?" Ian asked.

"Yes. Scoot," Emily said, ruffling their hair as they charged past.

Eden Stratton came in the kitchen door with a platter balanced in one hand and a baby in the crook of her other arm. She looked around the kitchen, spied Cherry—who apparently looked like the only one with nothing to do—and said, "Here. Take William before I drop all these honeybuns."

You'd have thought she'd yelled: *think fast!* Cherry practically leaped forward, her arms outstretched as though Eden was about to drop the baby instead of the buns. Which wasn't the case, of course. And she wasn't even certain why she reacted so strongly. But once she had that warm little bundle in her arms, everything within her softened. She pulled aside the blue blanket and gazed at the sweet baby boy.

"I could have taken the sweet rolls," she said to Eden once her heart settled. "You're starting to develop a bad habit of abandoning this baby into my care."

"Well, you've risen to the task quite nicely on both occasions." She grinned and set the buns on Emily's kitchen table. "Mercy, there are a lot of kids out there. And it's cold! But do you think any of them even notices?"

"Not when there are horses around," Emily said. She moved over to have a peek at the baby. "He's growing like a weed."

"Want him?" Cherry asked, thinking she ought not to hog the sweet thing.

"As much as I'd love to get my hands on him, they're a little messy at the moment." She raised her palms, showing a smear of mayonnaise. Had she been mixing the potato salad with her hands?

"Come sit," Hannah Malone urged, moving from her place by the kitchen counter where she'd been assembling condiments for the burgers. "And tell us how you're feeling."

"Still a little sore. My leg's healing, but the ribs are taking a little longer."

"Cryin' all night," Eden exclaimed. "I forgot about your poor ribs. Here, I'll take the baby. You sit."

Now that Eden had plucked the infant from her arms, Cherry was sorry to give him up. She sat at the kitchen table for lack of anything better to do, feeling as out of place in this room full of women as a skunk at a church picnic.

And as much as she felt uncomfortable, she equally wished that she could relax and fit in. She'd spent the majority of the past few years like one of the guys. Outdoors concentrating on cattle and feed and disease and endless repairs. It had been way too long since she'd had the luxury of girl talk and girl-friends.

The rest of the women in the kitchen didn't seem to feel any discomfort at all and chattered away, dragging Cherry into the conversation with ease.

"Did Hannah tell you the latest about her love-sick goat?" Dora asked, sitting at the table, holding her baby son, Ryan, in her lap.

Cherry shook her head, glanced over at Hannah, who shrugged.

"Everyone knows goats get bored and lonely when they're alone. That's why it's good to have at least two." Dora was happy to show off her goat knowledge. "That's what Lyle told us when Billy started moping and went off his feed."

"Well to be fair," Hannah said, "he *had* eaten an entire sheet off the clothesline. That could have accounted for his behavior."

Dora laughed. "He's so attached to Hannah—she's basically his other goat—and when she had Meredith he felt like she'd abandoned him, so he started moping."

"And eating the sheets," Hannah reminded again.

"That's when Wyatt called my brother. Lyle prescribed a companion goat—other than Hannah." Dora grinned when Hannah gave her a mock insulted look.

Cherry checked to see if Hannah was indeed insulted and was pretending not to be. Dora *had* sort of called her a goat. And she wondered why Hannah was even hanging sheets on the clothesline in the first place. Was her clothes dryer broken?

"Did you get another goat?" she asked.

"Yes. Her name is Willa. And if I'm not mistaken there will be little Billies and Willas in the near future."

Cherry smiled. "Baby goats are awfully cute."

"And what about your brother?" Eden asked Dora. "Any companions for him on the horizon?"

"Not that I know of—unless Cherry's interested? Lyle is a great catch. Filthy rich, veterinarian, above average in the looks department." Dora grinned. "Although I'm thinking Clay might have something to say about that. He's pretty much got you sewed up. Am I right?"

Cherry didn't want to have this conversation. According to Clay, everyone knew they were 'a thing'. For some reason, she didn't want to absolutely confirm the rumor. Instead of answering the question, she said, "I imagine my uncle and his pals have your brother in their sights. He should start worrying about his bachelor status—if he's of a mind to hang on to it."

"Oh, those old geezers. I love them!" Dora said with a laugh. "I've heard some scuttlebutt that Mildred and Opal are tryin' to horn in on the matchmaking activity."

"Heaven help your brother."

"Right? Who'd have thought this town was short on women and babies just a couple of years ago?"

"Speaking of those babies, where are the rest of y'alls kids?" Cherry asked.

"Wyatt has Meredith," Hannah said, "and Ian is outside with Nikki riding horses, I'm thinking."

"Ethan has Katie," Dora said, shifting Ryan in her lap.

"And Stony has Sarah," Eden added. "But since he's in charge of the horses—I mean that man *is* a horse whisperer—I imagine Clay or one of the other guys must have her. My husband is so good with these kids, he could have handled all three *and* the horses, but since William is still nursing, I decided to keep him with me." She gazed at the baby boy in her arms.

"You know I didn't know if I could even have kids." Eden directed her words toward Cherry since the other women in the room knew her story. "I have a condition called Adenomyosis—endometriosis of the uterus. I'm healthiest when I'm pregnant—which is why Sarah and William are so close in age, barely eleven months apart. Let me tell you, though. Having two babies in diapers is wearing me out a lot more than gully-washer periods and anemia."

"Are you planning to have more kids?" Cherry asked, astonishing herself once again. She *never* pried into other folk's business like this.

Kelly Hammond had just come through the door and had clearly heard part of the conversation. Cherry noticed the compassionate, yet uncertain look that passed between Eden and Kelly.

"Both Doctor Hammonds—Kelly *and* Chance—are keeping a close eye on me. I have everything my heart could ever desire in these three kids and Stony. And Stony is pressuring me to have the surgery."

"He's worried about you," Kelly said. "He's so crazy in love with you."

"I know. I don't know how I got so lucky. So, to answer your question, Cherry. I think that William is the last for us. After the first of the year, I'll probably have the hysterectomy."

Cherry automatically reached for Eden's hand, surprising herself and the other woman. It wasn't like her to act this way. *My gosh—prying, comforting. What would she do next? Join the church choir? Still, the thought of knowing you could not have any more children would be a difficult one to face. Even though Eden had three children—Nikki, who she hadn't given birth to, and two more whom she had—it would still mess with her emotions to have that ability taken away forever.*

Cherry should know.

She gave Eden's hand a squeeze and let go as Clay and Ethan came in the back door, each with a child riding on their shoulders—Ethan's daughter Katie, and Clay's niece Jolie.

"Oh, good," Emily said. "You men are just in time. Make yourselves useful and haul these platters of food outside."

Cherry reached for the plate of condiments Hannah had set on the table across from her.

"Nope," Emily said. "You're operating under a handicap. We'll send the guys for the rest of the food. Let's get these kids outside." Proving she'd done this more than once, Emily hooked a lasso-type rope through the trays of the twins' rolling seats and pulled them outside like a couple of little wagons.

The rest of the women and men scooped up children and whatever else they could carry and followed her out of the kitchen.

Clay, with Jolie on his shoulders, came over to the table and helped Cherry out of the chair.

"I'm good," she said, feeling embarrassed and inadequate because she wasn't operating at full capacity and helping like everyone else.

He winked at her. "No argument from me."

Her face heated. He was making a veiled reference to sex, she knew. If they'd been a true couple, she would have smacked him on the arm, admonished him to behave.

Instead, she felt uneasy. Everyone was making decisions for her, going around her, overruling her objections as though she didn't have a voice. It was starting to push her buttons, making her want to withdraw.

She looked at Clay, standing there with a grin on his face, unaware that anything was amiss. He was so sexy, especially with a little bitty four-year-old with chubby cheeks and blond, stubby pigtails riding on his shoulders.

Cherry wondered why she was suddenly confronted by so many babies. Baby animals and baby humans. It was almost a conspiracy. Making her face the one thing she'd always wanted and couldn't have. Reminding her that she was the wrong woman for Clay Callahan, a kind man who was born to be a father—a family man.

~

CHERRY PULLED on warm clothes and made her way through the house, the sight of the festive tree barely registering. After spending the previous day with all the happy families and watching Clay laugh and cart around toddlers on his shoulders, Cherry's heart was heavy.

It didn't help that John and Jenny White Cloud had taken the kittens home with them. She didn't realize how much she would miss the sweet little furballs.

She felt old and used up. She'd already been through a fifteen-year marriage that had been like living through a war zone. She didn't trust the longevity of relationships. The PTSD that winged out of nowhere when she least expected was a flaw she need not inflict on a partner. There were no babies on her horizon, which meant that if she continued her relationship with Clay, he would be doomed to the same fate.

How could she do that to him?

He'd told her he wanted to adopt children as Fred Callahan had done for him and his brothers. But why shouldn't he have the best of both worlds? It would be a crying shame if he never fathered a child. He was the type of man who should have a whole passel of children running around. He had a heart full of love to give. And she was being selfish by holding on, taking time away from the path that he was truly meant to follow.

And her skittishness would eventually get on his nerves. What then? She had a whole closet full of flaws that made the future and the certainty of peace a turkey shoot.

She had to let him go. Seeing all the happy couples yesterday had solidified that decision for her. Clay wanted what his brothers and friends had. And she could not give that to him.

She wanted to go hide under the covers and cry. Instead, she squared her shoulders and pulled on her mantle of aloofness, which had served her well over the years.

She'd had years of practice at acting. She'd had to in order to survive life with Dell. Now, she was about to put on an academy award-winning performance.

But there would be no award for her.

She went outside and started the truck, letting the heater warm up the cab while she loaded the bed with various tools, including her crowbar so she could make sure the ice was broken in all the watering holes and troughs. She saw that the hay wagon was missing, realized that Clay had it. She checked the hitch on the back of the Ford, made sure the right ball was attached.

She'd be bringing back the wagon herself.

Because she intended to send Clay home.

$\mathcal{C}$lay knew something was brewing. When they'd gotten home from Cheyenne's last night, they'd made love with a bittersweet desperation that had rocked his world, yet filled him with dread.

His gut clenched when he saw her blue Ford coming up the slushy path toward him. He suddenly felt like he was standing in the middle of a stampede with no exit. Helpless to stop what was about to happen.

Cherry was a stubborn woman. It was one of the things he loved about her. It was also one of the things that gave him the most grief.

He laid aside the pitchfork he'd been using to toss hay into the bull's pen, and jumped off the tailgate.

"Hey." He met her as she alighted from the driver's side door. "What are you doing out here?"

"Relieving you." She pulled on her gloves.

"Who said I needed relief?" He didn't dare take his eyes off of her, felt like if he did, she'd disappear into a puff of smoke. Why couldn't he read her better?

"Clay, you can't keep working my ranch forever. I appreciate everything you've done, but it's time I took over."

"What's this all about?"

"I don't know what you mean."

He reached out abruptly, turned her to face him.

He should have expected the flinch, swore at himself for forgetting. He dropped his hand. "Are you kicking me out?"

"Don't be silly. I'm just saying that I can do my own chores."

"And I'm saying that you're not ready."

That clearly got her back up. Tough, he thought. He was holding on by a thread.

"I think I know my own body, Clay."

"Yeah, well, if you recall, I know it pretty well, too."

Cherry's heart did a little jig. She'd known this wasn't going to be easy. She'd miscalculated, though, big time. She wasn't one to deliberately hurt someone else. And that's what she was doing to Clay. She could tell by his stiff stance, the tension in his jaw. She was handling this all wrong. But, darn it all, she didn't know how else to do it, to convince him that he needed to get on with his life.

"What's this really about, Cherry?"

She leaned against his tailgate, wrapped her arms around her body, as much to keep from reaching for him as to keep warm.

"I guess I realized something yesterday when we were at Cheyenne's. I saw you with the kids, and you're a natural. You deserve to have a family, Clay. That's something I can't give you."

"Bull. We've covered this before."

His mounting anger made her nervous, but she stood her ground. "I know you said it didn't matter. But that's how you feel *now*. We're brand new, Clay. We've only been together a few weeks—"

"I think you know I've been in love with you for a lot longer than a few weeks."

She sucked in a breath. Why had he pulled out the love word now? Didn't he know this was breaking her heart?

Swallowing hard, she continued as though he hadn't spoken. "I went through close to fifteen years of hell. I didn't tell you the part where Dell kicked me in the stomach and damaged my spleen. That's when the doctor in the emergency room told me I might never have children. I didn't have that confirmed, but clearly I never got pregnant."

"Damnit to hell, Cherry." He reached for her, to comfort her or himself, she wasn't sure. But she stepped back.

"That's the thing, Clay. In a new relationship, everyone is on their best behavior. But when the newness wears off, when the sex isn't so shiny and urgent, true feelings come out."

"Are you actually saying you think I might end up being like Dell?"

"I don't think so...I'm not sure what I'm saying. But I do know that you can't be certain that you won't want kids. You say you don't now, but there's no way either of us can know if you'll change your mind. If you'll resent being tied to me several years down the road when I can't give you the one thing you need."

"When did I ever say that was the one thing I needed?"

"You didn't have to. It's clear to see."

"Not every man feels the need to grow a kid from his own seed. I happen to be one of those men."

"I wish I could believe that. And I do believe that you feel that way right this minute. It's down the road that I can't trust. Clay, I know what broken dreams feel like. I know what it's like to be stuck with the wrong person. I'm afraid I'm that wrong person for you."

"I resent that you're making that decision for me. There's nothing about you that I don't want." He shoved his hands deep into his pockets, as though he was trying to respect her space but didn't trust himself. "I don't know how to convince you of that."

His sadness and frustration were breaking her heart. She cupped his cheek, pressed her hand over his chest for an instant. "I'm sorry, Clay. And thank you for helping me with the ranch and taking care of me. I *am* grateful. But it's time for you to head for your own ranch and get on with your life."

"You don't mean that."

"Yes, I think I do."

Clay felt like the top of his head was about to blow off, like a million angry wasps were traveling from his stomach through his chest, stinging their way to his brain, making him want to bellow like a wounded bull.

He wanted to argue with her—*make* her see his point of view, his love. But like her subtle flinches, she'd likely view the strength of his emotions as bullying, as him insisting on having his way. Never mind that his was the *right* way, the right decision. He had to respect her boundaries. It was the hardest thing he'd ever done.

Closing his eyes, he gave a slight nod. He wasn't sure his heart would survive. "You know where to find me."

And with that, he slammed the tailgate shut, got in the truck, and drove away.

~

IT HAD BEEN MORE than a week since she'd sent Clay home—

nine days to be exact—and Cherry felt the agony of that loss every single day. He hadn't returned the horses she was being paid to board. She knew it had nothing to do with money and everything to do with making her life easier. He was still doing that—trying to take care of her from afar.

The festive lights on her tree reminded her that Christmas Eve was only three days away. She should have taken down the decorations, but couldn't bring herself to do it. For the first time in more years that she cared to count, she'd been looking forward to the holidays. She'd had a taste of community, holiday spirit, and love and been too afraid to accept it. What the heck was wrong with her?

She'd just finished a quick lunch when she glanced out the kitchen window and saw Hannah Malone's SUV pull into the yard, its huge knobby tires leaving wide tracks in the muddy snow. The other woman got out of the vehicle but didn't have any kids with her.

Cherry opened the kitchen door. Interesting that the neighbors now came to the back door like true friends. They didn't go around to the front like company. Her fears that everyone would be mad at her for hurting Clay were not being realized.

"Hi," Hannah said. "I'm checking up on you."

"Come on in. Can I get you some coffee?"

"No, I just wanted to make sure you weren't over here pining."

Cherry smiled, raised her brows. "Why would I be doing that?"

"Girl, this is a very small town and you know how things work. It's no secret that you sent Clay away. And that man *is* pining, I can tell you that right now."

Cherry closed her eyes, sat at the table. She desperately wanted to weep. "I didn't mean to hurt him."

"I know you didn't."

"It's just...how much did Clay tell you?"

"Not a thing, really. Just that he loves you and that your marriage taught you not to trust."

He hadn't betrayed her confidence. Why had she even considered that he would? Clay was an honorable man.

She realized that if she was going to have friends, she needed to be a friend as well. And that meant opening up about her secrets. It was time to get it all out in the open, to face the consequences of people's opinions.

She got up and poured two mugs of coffee, just to give herself something to do, then sat with Hannah at the table and told her the truth about Dell.

Hannah had tears in her eyes. "I just hate that you bore all this on your own, that you didn't think you could reach out even to your uncle."

Cherry shrugged. "Shame is a powerful motivator. It colored every one of my decisions, how I felt about myself—what I *allowed*. That's hard to admit."

Hannah reached for Cherry's hand. "I can relate. I wasn't beaten and abused like you, but I was lied to and cheated on. My husband had affairs and left me when he found out I was pregnant with Meredith. I could have gone into myself and decided never to trust another man, and no one would have faulted me for it. But look what I would have missed. A wonderful, caring, faithful man who would accept my children as his own and love me the way every woman ever dreams of being loved. You have that opportunity staring you in the face, Cherry. Clay Callahan loves you beyond reason.

He is a kind and gentle man. Maybe he's bossy, but it's out of love. It's not to control you."

"You know I didn't like you when you came here," Cherry said to Hannah. She could hardly believe this particular woman had become her ally.

Hannah smiled. "I know. You were a little sweet on Wyatt."

"Not really. He's the epitome of what I wanted, but I didn't want *him*. Sounds totally ridiculous, right?

"Of course not. It's just that he wasn't the right man."

"I know. I'm so scared."

"Well, that club's not exclusive. Putting your future in someone else's hands and trusting them to treasure it is scary for all of us. But if you don't take a leap, you'll stay stuck. There are second chances and happy endings. I'm a prime example. As for the children aspect, take a good look at the people in this town. Wyatt adopted my two kids and you'd never know they weren't from his own DNA. Katie isn't Dora's biological daughter, but she couldn't love that little girl more if she was. Nikki was Stony's goddaughter—look at them. Cheyenne and Emily —she was a surrogate for her sister and brother-in-law. Emily's brother-in-law was actually Cheyenne's brother, so they're both technically aunt and uncle, but you won't find finer, more loving parents. Dan and Amy adopted Shayna when her mother died. Grant formally adopted Jolie. The men in this town are loving and kind and they'll go to the mat for you. Don't assign qualities to Clay that just aren't there. He's a good man, Cherry."

Hannah stood and gently touched Cherry's shoulder. Her eyes were kind and compassionate. "Reach for your happy ending. If you can. I certainly won't discount your very real emotions and fears. But you have a choice."

When Hannah let herself out the kitchen door, Hope came

in and laid her head in Cherry's lap. Joy leaped onto the chair and nosed her way into the circle. Cherry gathered them both in. Could she actually allow herself a second chance? Should she?

~

SNOW FELL like magical fairy dust on Christmas Eve. Cherry forced herself to get in the truck and drive to town, even though she was sorely tempted to fall back on her standard excuses and stay home. It wasn't easy to arrive solo and figure out where she fit in. Or even if she *did* fit in.

The annual holiday tree ceremony would be starting soon, right after Pastor Dan wrapped up his Christmas Eve service at the church. The order of the festivities had changed a bit this year since Pastor Dan and Amy now had two children. Cherry had deliberately made a point of missing the church service and now felt guilty. She reasoned that she'd have felt extra conspicuous if she'd gone to the church. Better to wait until folks headed over to the square where the children would each get to choose a gift from under the tree. That way, she could mingle with the crowd under the cover of darkness and not feel like such an odd duck. Cherry hadn't been part of this ritual in the past. And she wasn't sure why she was going tonight—except she was desperate to see Clay.

She hadn't seen him since the afternoon she'd broken things off. She kept thinking about what Hannah said. *If you don't take a leap, you'll stay stuck.* And she didn't want to stay stuck. She wanted to move forward.

In the center of the square, surrounded by the courthouse, the church, the clinic, and the veterinarian's office stood a lighted gazebo and the twenty-foot tall tree, its lights shining bright enough to guide an airplane through the fog—or perhaps Santa's sleigh. The smell of cinnamon, popcorn, and chocolate mingled with the scent of pine and frigid air. Voices murmured as Christmas music floated softly on the air. The sights and smells and sounds made her feel young and happy and hopeful.

And loved.

Even though everyone knew there had been a rift between her and Clay, her newly formed friendships hadn't dissolved like she'd thought they would. People still called, still invited her to join in. Like tonight. She'd received six phone calls— two of which had been from Clay's family members—with offers to come get her if she didn't want to arrive alone.

Mildred and Opal had threatened to get out the Buick and stage a friendly kidnapping if she didn't agree to come on her own. Cherry shuddered at the thought. Not only because they lived right there on Main Street and didn't need to drive anywhere—but the idea of those two ladies behind the wheel of a vehicle on snowy roads was something she didn't want to consider.

They were so dang sweet to insist, though.

Friends. She had them. Good friends. The kind who had your back. And she suspected they would have had her back a whole lot sooner if she'd have just let them in.

She'd wasted a lot of years trapped in fear and tattered self-esteem.

She saw Clay through an opening in the throng of people and her heart leaped. He was so tall, so still, his white hat towering above the crowd, making him easy to spot. Or was it just her? She imagined every woman here felt the same about their man—that they could easily spot them in a crowd.

Was he her man? Lord, the thought scared her.

Could she willingly go down that road again?

In that moment, he looked up, as though drawn from an invisible force, and caught sight of her. He went absolutely still. He said something to his brother, who was standing next to him, then came toward her, his steady gaze holding hers, delighting her.

At least he was meeting her halfway. She hadn't been sure after the way they'd parted. She'd insisted that they were over. Now, she was pretty sure she was fixing to ask for a second chance. Did she dare hope? Was it selfish of her?

He stopped in front of her. "Merry Christmas."

She smiled. "Not yet. It's only Christmas Eve."

"Ah, but Santa comes Christmas Eve. I'm glad you came."

"Mildred and Opal threatened dire consequences if I didn't."

His smile was so charming, so familiar. So loved. "That the only reason you showed?"

She shook her head. "I think I was kind of hoping I'd see you."

"Ditto." He pulled an envelope from his pocket and handed it to her. "This is for you. I was going to bring it by in the morning. I wasn't sure you'd be here tonight."

She felt guilty that she didn't have a gift for him. "Clay, you shouldn't have—"

"Just open it."

She did, carefully lifting the flap, pulling the sheet of paper out. He activated the flashlight on his cell phone and held it up so she could see what she was reading.

A reconveyance document. With her address on it.

She frowned, searched for a date. He couldn't have had this recorded in the short time between when he'd left her ranch and now could he? When had he done this? *How* had he done this?

He mistook her silence for confusion and said, "I paid off your loan."

Her heart began to pound and thought after irrational thought tumbled through her head.

"Why would you do that without consulting me?"

"Cherry, it's a good thing, not a bad one."

"You took the decision out of my hands. Once again, you're trying to control me."

His jaw tightened. He made every effort not to lose his temper. "I'm not trying to control you. I'm trying to make your life easier. I'm trying to make *our* lives easier, damnit. I love you. I don't want to see you work yourself half to death and struggle when I've got more money than I know what to do with. I'm not investing in your ranch. It's all yours. Free and clear. It's my gift to you. No strings attached. Hell, I don't even have to come with the bargain." He threw up his hands and took a step toward her.

She instinctively stepped back.

He swore. "See, that right there is something I can't compete with. I can't prove to you that I'm not like that piece of shit you were married to. I'm human. I lose my temper when I don't get my way, or when I hit my thumb with a hammer—hell, lots of reasons. I just don't know how to prove to you that I'd never hurt you."

He took a deep breath, closed his eyes for a moment, then turned to walk away.

Cherry's hands shook. She couldn't catch her breath, couldn't find her voice. She *needed* to find her voice. Dang it, she had to try. Because Hannah was right. He was her second chance. He'd proved time and again that she could trust him.

His love was different. Yes, he had a possessive streak, but he was devoted and reasonable. He was kind. There was nothing similar between him and Dell.

Even if he was bossy. That didn't mean he wanted to strip her of her independence. And she'd *told* him how important it was to own her ranch free and clear again. Of course he would move mountains—or at least shift a few funds in his bank account—to make that a reality for her. That's the kind of man he was.

Over the past few weeks, he'd showed her what it was like to be a *team*. It's what she'd always wanted. To be part of a loving unit where she and her mate worked together toward their goals and their future. A teammate who helped carry the load in the family. Like Hannah and Wyatt. Dora and Ethan. Abbe and Grant. Eden and Stony. Uncle Ozzie and her late Aunt Vanessa.

Hadn't he proved that to her over and over these past few weeks as he'd done her chores for her, then worked alongside her when she'd objected strenuously? When he'd stayed up to help her feed the kittens around the clock? Cooked her meals and kept her warm and brought her fancy coffee makers? Left her notes so she'd know he'd fed the dogs?

He didn't just speak his feelings. He showed them. And actions surely did speak louder than words.

"Clay...don't go."

His steps faltered. He didn't turn around, but neither did he move farther away.

"I'm an idiot," she said to his back.

She saw his shoulders rise and fall.

This time he *did* turn around. Slowly. "In the interest of self-preservation—*mine*—I'm hesitant to agree or disagree with that statement." His voice was soft.

She took the first step toward him. It was time to meet him more than halfway. "Since I said it, you're welcome to agree."

"And if I were to … agree," he said carefully, hope filling his eyes when he saw her smile, "what specific behavior would you be referring to?"

She laughed out loud at that. "Lord, there are so many. We'd be here all night if you wanted me to list them. Let's start with the most obvious. I love you."

His brows shot up, shifting his hat. "And that makes you an idiot?"

She stopped in front of him. "Not recognizing or trusting is the dumb part. The loving part is kind of scary, but pretty nice."

He reached out, lightly skimmed his fingertips up her arms, over her shoulders, her neck, cupped her cheeks.

"I'm going to kiss you before we go any farther. You okay with that?"

She nodded, and he lowered his head. His lips were warm and gentle, so reverent and so clearly filled with love. The emotions emanated from him in tangible waves.

It wasn't just Clay. The whole town had been trying to show her that she was part of them. Community spirit. They'd drawn her in against her best efforts to stay isolated. Because deep down, she didn't want isolation. She wanted family, love, friends. But most of all, she wanted Clay.

She broke the kiss, looked up into his eyes. "Thank you for this." She indicated the envelope. "You've given me so much," she said. "What can I give you?"

"Just you. You're all I want."

"But…babies? Are you sure—"

"Sweetheart, I don't need children from my own DNA.

Fred Callahan taught me that. I don't know who my biological father is, and I don't care. My life is full and fulfilling. And that's because of Fred Callahan. I'd like to be that for another child—maybe several children. But we'll make that decision in time. Together. For now and forever, all I need is you. And I need you more than the air I breathe."

"You're my dream come true," she said. "And I'd love to explore adoption with you. Lord knows I'm not opposed to taking in strays. Look at all the extra animals who come my way. Between the two of us, I think we could be a child in need's hope. Like Pastor Dan and Amy are for Shayna."

"And like my dad was for Ethan, Grant, and me."

"I wish I'd met him."

"He would have loved you. Marry me, Cherry?"

She never thought she would be in this place again. "Yes. I'll marry you."

He whooped and lifted her right off the ground, twirling her in a dizzying, exuberant circle. A crowd of friends and family had gathered around.

"She said yes!" Clay shouted, as laughter and applause rang through the night.

Love and healing and miracles. The epitome of Christmas in Shotgun Ridge. As she melted into Clay's kiss, Cherry's heart swelled. Her cup was definitely overflowing.

∼

OZZIE PEYTON GAZED up at the star atop the Christmas tree, noticed that it glowed a little brighter. His eyes were wet with emotions, which could have accounted for the little prisms he saw glowing around the star, but he knew better. He knew how to spot a miracle when he saw one.

And he knew that his Vanessa was watching, smiling down on all of them. She would be so pleased that Cherry had found Clay.

That's right, love. You hear that? We've done it again. I'm pretty sure you had some help from the Man upstairs, and we surely appreciate it. I trust you'll pass along our appreciation. This niece of ours deserves the very best. And Clay Callahan is the best, you bet.

Yes sir-ee, this is a happy Christmas, indeed. Merry Christmas, my love.

*S*pringtime in Montana was the perfect time for a wedding. Cherry trees scattered their fat pink blossoms over the verdant expanse of lawn between the house and barn. In a few minutes, she'd be walking along that flower strewn pathway to meet her groom.

She hadn't wanted a fussy wedding. That wasn't her style.

So, the ceremony was taking place in the newly renovated barn. Clay had trailered her animals over to the Callahan and Son's farm—much the same as he'd done that first day when she'd been hurt by the bull.

As an engagement gift, he'd bought back Wyatt's half of Casanova so that she had one hundred percent ownership once again. The way he tossed his money around was taking some getting used to. She still sold semen to Wyatt—which wasn't much different than their purchase agreement. But owning Casanova outright meant something to her. It was hard to explain. But Clay had understood her need. And although she didn't imagine Clay gave him much choice, she knew that Wyatt understood as well. This time, that sweet bull—who was sort of like family, much to Clay's bewilderment—would be handled correctly. Her parents had given her Casanova to ensure her future. Dell had nearly squandered away that future with his drinking and depression.

But she had a second chance now. And looking around her, what a second chance that was.

The changes in her ranch were amazing—and even more astonishing was the speed with which those changes had taken place. The barn was only the tip of the iceberg. Clay had money and was determined to spend it on their future. Together, they'd designed plans for a new ranch house, planning to use this one as a guest house for the many visitors they would have over the years—especially her family. They'd already broken ground and she could see part of the framing from her place here at the bedroom window.

In a few months, they'd have a perfect view of the barn from their new front porch so they could watch over things. Everything would be brand new and top-of-the line. Her dream home. Cherry would never have to worry about turning on a faucet with a wrench or watching YouTube videos on how to repair a toaster. Clay was meticulous when it came to upkeep and progress. Although pride had her insisting that she contribute equally—both financially and in sweat equity. She didn't have endlessly deep pockets like Clay did, but she thrived on hard work and her registered herd was growing and flourishing. She and Clay were a team. And that felt wonderful.

She pressed a hand to her flat stomach, felt the delicate beading of her wedding dress beneath her palm. Nerves? She'd been feeling a little off lately, and knew it wasn't from the bachelorette night. Who would have thought she'd have a bachelorette party?

"You doing okay there, sis?"

Cherry turned and opened her arms to her sister, Brooke. "Yes, I'm so much better than okay." Clay had flown her home right after Christmas—in Abbe's Baron because it was faster and he'd just wanted to get his hands on the controls, she'd suspected—and she'd told her family everything. There had been guilt on both sides with the unburdening, but seeing her happy had smoothed things over. "Where's Mama?"

"I'm right here, darlin'." Joanne Peyton came into the bedroom and stopped, her eyes tearing up. "Look at both of my girls. You are both stunning." Like their mother, both Cherry and Brooke had natural red hair and petite figures. Joanne's mother-of-the-bride dress was a soft lavender where Brooke's was a sunny yellow. Cherry had wanted happy colors, springtime colors. The color of renewal and awakening, of healthy buds that foretold of a rich and abundant future.

Her own dress was simple yet elegant. A slim column of off-white satin and beads. Beneath that simplicity were *very* sexy undergarments and brown cowboy boots with ivory carvings. A denim jacket hung on the back of the door in case it got cool later on this evening.

"Mercy," Joanne said, "there's been a steady stream of women and children in and out of this house all morning. It's a wonder any of us have gotten dressed."

Cherry laughed. "Crazy, isn't it? I don't think I've ever had this many genuine friends, even when I was in high school."

"It makes me happy." Joanne walked over and enfolded both her daughters in her arms. "I grieved when you moved away from Texas, worried that you'd spend too much time alone. If I'd only known—"

"Mama," Cherry interrupted, sharing a look with her

sister. "Only happy thoughts today, okay?" Joanne was having some trouble releasing her heartache and guilt that one of her special chicks had suffered.

"Yes, you're so right, hon. And they are very happy thoughts. You have quite a support system here in Montana. And I tell you what. I'm not used to this highfalutin lifestyle. Being escorted here by Dora's granddaddy in his Lear jet was something I never thought I'd experience in my lifetime."

Cherry laughed. "These Callahans do like their aircraft."

"Well, technically, I believe that jet belongs to a Watkins." Joanne smoothed her hand over Brooke's shoulder, then Cherry's. Fussing as mothers tended to do when filled with so much love and pride. It fairly radiated out of her. "I do think I'm a little jealous though—I mean, Mildred and Opal actually told me they considered themselves surrogate mothers! As if you don't already have a perfectly fine one of your own."

Cherry drew her mother more closely into their circle. "And you are *so* fine, Mama. No one will ever replace you."

"Oh, I do know that. And I don't mean a thing by it. I'm truly thrilled for you, because once and for all, I know you'll be okay. You'll be loved and cherished—not just by Clay, but by this entire town. I've seen that first hand these last few months."

That was so true. Cherry couldn't believe how many girl-friends she'd acquired. Two of them—Dora and Abbe—would formally be sisters-in-law within the hour. The rest, Hannah, Eden, Emily, Kelly, Amy, even Iris, Mildred, and Opal. Not only did she have sister-friends, as her mama had just said, she had surrogate mothers as well. And though nobody could ever replace Joanne, having the older women in town cluck over her was icing on her beautiful cake, especially since Mama lived over fifteen hundred miles away on a working ranch that didn't allow for spur of the moment travel. Any visits would have to be panned in advance—something Cherry would need to arrange with her family very soon.

"Are the guests all at the barn?" Brooke asked.

"I believe so." Joanne kissed Cherry on the cheek. "Dora herded the last of the kids out of here a few minutes ago. One cute little thing slipped out with Joy under his arm, so no telling what's in store for us at this service."

Cherry grinned. She was fine with Hope and Joy attending the service. They were family. They'd just add to the special ambiance. "Okay, then. I guess that's our cue?"

"Yes, and I'm happy that your sister suggested that she and I be the ones to escort you to the wedding. If I had my way, we'd get you all the way to the altar."

"Well, we don't want to hurt Daddy and Uncle Ozzie's feelings," Brooke said. "So this was the best compromise. When my girls are grown and getting married, I surely intend to be on their arm to present them to their soulmates. I never understood the tradition that gave all that joy to the daddies." Since Brooke's daughters were barely ten and eight, she had a ways to go.

Linking arms with Mama and her sister, Cherry gave one last nervous glance in the mirror and headed out with them across the lawn.

Ozzie and her father met them just outside the door of the barn, and each offered her an arm. Ozzie had insisted that he be part of the ceremony since he figured his matchmaking skills had contributed to hers and Clay's union—even thought he'd told anyone who would listen that it was actually his sweet Vanessa's doing. Cherry halfway believed him.

Pastor Dan came in to stand next to Clay and Ethan, his laughter preceding him. The man was so full of joy, it was contagious. A year ago, she wouldn't have thought any of this —especially the soul tickling joy—was possible.

"Ready to do this?" Bill Peyton asked.

"Very ready."

Bill and Ozzie, brothers who looked astonishingly alike, both had moisture in their eyes.

Joanne and Brooke preceded them down the aisle.

CLAY'S NERVES were standing on edge. These last few months had been the best of his life, and he'd counted the hours until he could make it official, make her his wife. If he'd had his way, he would have married her on Christmas Eve.

But ever practical, Cherry had wanted to wait until the calves dropped, until there was a good break in the seasons of ranching so her family could make plans to be here for at least a week.

He looked out at their friends and family seated in rented white chairs, waiting for the bride to arrive.

"Breathe, bro," Ethan said in his ear. "It's time."

He took the suggestion, surprised at his nerves. Everyone looked relaxed and happy. His sisters-in-law had decorated the barn in spring colors of yellow and lavender as Cherry had requested. Daises, lilacs, white roses, and lilies adorned every available surface turning the barn into a springtime meadow. They'd brought over a piano, and Kelly Hammond began to play "Storybook Love" from the movie *The Princess Bride.*

It was a non-traditional wedding and deserved a non-traditional song. And theirs was a storybook love. Complete with a happy ending that would last until the end of their time.

At that moment, he saw her standing in the open doorway of the barn, and his heart jolted so hard he felt dizzy. Emotion flooded him, so fiercely and quickly he nearly dropped to his knees. This woman, his every heart's desire, was about to become his wife.

Her red hair flowed around her face and past her shoulders. None of that fussy up do stuff for this woman—although there were curls she didn't normally mess with. Her slim, athletic body created the perfect frame for the off-white dress that hugged her curves and flowed to the ground. Cowboy boots peeked from the hem with each step she took.

His eyes never left hers as she came down the aisle between the rows of chairs holding their friends and family. At last she stopped in front of him, an incredibly soft, reassuring smile barely curving her lips. He let out the breath he hadn't been aware of holding.

"You are the most beautiful woman I have ever laid eyes on."

"Here now," Ozzie scolded mildly. "There's an order to these here weddings. It's not your turn for talking until Bill and I agree to give her away."

"And do you?" he asked with a smile, his eyes still holding Cherry's.

"Well, I think that's where I'll just step in," Pastor Dan said with a jovial laugh. "Who gives this lovely woman to be married to this man?"

"He could have at least added 'handsome'," Clay murmured.

Pastor Dan laughed.

Ozzie and Bill said in unison, "We *all* do."

"The whole town, in fact, you bet," Ozzie added to a ripple of laughter.

Clay was happy with the laughter. He planned to spend the rest of his life making sure she laughed and felt safe and loved.

He took her hands, lightly pressed his lips to hers.

From the corner of his eye, he saw that Ozzie was about to object, but Mildred Bagley slapped a hand over his mouth.

Pastor Dan raised his brows. "Ready for me, or y'all want to just carry on?"

"Be our guest," Clay said.

Dan went through the standard wedding vows, but Clay barely heard him. His sole focus was on Cherry. Seeing the happiness shining from her eyes was everything to him.

He promised to love her until the end of time, and she did the same. When his brother handed him the ring, he slipped it on her hand and saw moisture fill her eyes. She hadn't wanted a fancy diamond ring set because her hands were so often in and out of gloves. He'd gotten her a flat band with channel diamonds that sparkled but was at the same time unfussy enough for a woman like Cherry.

When Dan pronounced them husband and wife, Clay knew he was luckiest man in the world. He didn't have to wait for Dan's permission to kiss her, which earned them more laughter and sighs from the crowd. She was like the sweetest magnet, drawing him to her.

He raised his head to look down at his wife. "You are all I'll ever need or want. I am so in love with you."

"About that...um—"

"Sugar, you're making me a little scared here. You just said 'I do' and now?"

She smiled. "I might should have said *we* do."

He frowned. "We, as in...? He let the sentence trail off so she'd hopefully fill in the blank.

"Our baby and me."

He went very still. "I thought—"

"Me, too. But I've peed on four sticks this morning and they all say positive. We're going to have a baby."

He lifted her right off the ground, kissed her with all the love in his soul. The congregation roared and clapped. Joy, who'd been sitting politely in Ian Malone's lap wearing a delicate string of lavender flowers around her neck, leaped down and charged through the crowd like a maniac. Hope, who'd been laying at Ian's feet, shot off after her, clearly desperate to rein in the mannerless puppy.

The laughter, chaos, and fun only added to the perfectness of Cherry's day.

Under the cover of the clatter, Clay said in her ear, "You're enough, Cherry. You know that, right? You always have been and always will be enough."

"Yes. Thankfully, I *do* know that. And I also know that we both have enough love to invite this baby into our lives." She pressed her hand to her abdomen and he placed his over it. "You are my heart's desire, Clay. I couldn't be happier. I'd given up on the idea of ever being a mom. And now I have that chance. You've given me so much. And now, you've given me our child."

"I'd still like to adopt some day."

"Me, too. I mean, you're building a house big enough to accommodate a village. We'll need to fill those rooms. And I can't think of anything I'd love more than to fill them with children and animals."

"We're going to have a good life together."

"The best. Just like in the storybooks."

And she believed it.

~

MISSED any of the Shotgun Ridge titles? All can be read as stand-alone books. Pick a bachelor...or all of them!

THE RANCHER'S MAIL-ORDER-BRIDE—Wyatt Malone
THE PLAYBOY'S OWN MISS PRIM—Ethan Callahan
THE HORSEMAN'S CONVENIENT WIFE—Stony Stratton
CHEYENNE'S LADY—Cheyenne Bodine
THE DOCTOR'S INSTANT FAMILY—Chance Hammond
PREACHER'S IN-NAME-ONLY WIFE—Dan Lucas
SHOTGUN RIDGE—Grant Callahan
CHRISTMAS IN SHOTGUN RIDGE—Clay Callahan

~

WANT to know the latest Mindy Neff news? Join her email list for giveaways, advance reader copies and book news: www.-mindyneff.com.

ALSO BY MINDY NEFF

Love Cowboys? Try Mindy's Texas Sweethearts series.

As young girls, they vowed to be best friends forever—a promise they've kept through happiness and heartbreak! Now these four Texas Sweethearts are all turning thirty. In spite of busy lives, full-time careers, and an assortment of beloved animals and meddling townsfolk, true love is destined to surprise each one of them in the magical little world of their own hometown.

They've sworn they *aren't* looking for love...aren't those famous last words!

COURTED BY A COWBOY (Book 1)

SURPRISED BY A BABY (Book 2)

RESCUED BY A RANCHER (Book 3)

TEMPTED BY A TEXAN (Book 4)

Stand Alone Titles

THE COWBOY IS A DADDY

A FAMILY MAN

ADAM'S KISS

THE BAD BOY NEXT DOOR

ABOUT MINDY

Mindy Neff is the *USA Today* and *Wall Street Journal* bestselling author of over thirty novels and novellas. Her books have won the National Reader's Choice Award, the Orange Rose Award of Excellence, the Romantic Times Career Achievement Award, and the Romantic Times Reviewer's Choice Award, as well as W.I.S.H awards for outstanding hero, and two prestigious RITA® nominations.

To learn more about Mindy and her books, visit her website at: http://mindyneff.com/ and join her email/newsletter list for new and upcoming releases, news and giveaways and advance reading/review copies.

Join Mindy's email list: www.mindyneff.com
Follow Mindy on BookBub
Join Mindy on Facebook:
Join Mindy's Facebook reader group:
Email Mindy at: mindy@mindyneff.com
Follow Mindy on Twitter:

CPSIA information can be obtained
at www.ICGtesting.com
Printed in the USA
FSHW012258121221
86868FS